Seven Tails of Christmas

Rob Edwards

Seven Tails of Christmas

All characters in this book are fictitious, and any resemblance to any person, living or dead, is purely coincidental.

No portion of this publication may be reproduced, stored in a retrieval system, or delivered in any form, by any means without the written permission of the author or publisher.

Copyright © 2019 Rayn Media

All rights reserved.

ISBN-13: 978-1-7340656-0-2: ebook

ISBN-13: 978-1-7340656-1-9: paperback

Seven Tails of Christmas

For Dayna Marie

1

Cheri Porter passed away on January 8th, at the age of 56. It was a Tuesday.

The irony of it all was not lost on her broken-hearted husband. Ellis Porter knew his wife hated Tuesdays. She always called it a worthless nothing of a day. "It doesn't matter how you feel about Mondays, at least it's the start of something," she used to say. "Wednesday is 'hump-day,' Thursday means it's almost done, and then comes 'thank God, it's Friday.' But Tuesday is a completely unremarkable day. Nothing good has ever happened on a Tuesday." If anybody tried to argue that point with her, she would just mention that "Black Tuesday" kicked off the Great Depression, and that 9-11-2001 was also a Tuesday. Cheri won the argument every time.

Ellis shivered and pulled his fleece blanket—Iowa Hawkeyes— a little tighter over his shoulder. He sat in the recliner that angled toward both the flat-screen in his living room, and the sliding glass door that opened to the Zen backyard garden he and Cheri had worked so hard on. The garden was a labor of love, and a reminder of their trip to Japan. It was one of their favorite trips, and the peaceful bliss of the Japanese gardens was one of the main reasons they loved it so. The Porter version had stone walkways winding through well-trimmed bushes, several rock sculptures, and a koi-less koi pond. They had just planted the bushes and were ready to shop for the fish when the pain in her hip started—the pain that was ultimately diagnosed as stage 4 uterine cancer. Ellis had kept it up nicely while Cheri was going through chemo. But since her passing, the bushes became overgrown and wiry, and weeds overtook the stone in the walkways. Ironically, the place they had envisioned as peaceful and serene, was now oppressively silent without his wife to share it with.

Ellis felt the ginger cat wind in and around his ankles, rubbing her whiskers up and down his calves. Smiling, he reached down, and picked up the tabby he and Cheri had rescued. "I get the hint, Strawberry. Come on up." He set Strawberry in his lap and scratched under her chin, instantly revving the loud purr motor. Off in the corner, Rhubarb, their miniature border collie, and also a rescued pet, lifted his lazy head and looked over like he was missing out on something.

Ellis reached a hand down by the floor and snapped his fingers. "Come here, boy. I've got some for you too."

It looked like work for Rhubarb to raise himself to all fours, but he managed, wearily padded over next to Ellis's chair, and lay back down. Ellis scratched the old dog under his chin, realizing that both the cat and the dog, whom Cheri had named after her favorite pie, would probably be joining her soon. Perhaps they, too, would go on a Tuesday.

Ellis looked out at the cold, gray evening, and the barren trees and bushes as they shivered in the brisk December wind. He thought back on the year of the firsts he'd had to endure since Cheri passed.

It seemed like her funeral had just ended and it was Valentine's Day. It was the first one, since two years before they were married, that they didn't share chocolate-covered strawberries and champagne. Cheri was a stickler for tradition and she would never let February 14th pass without doing it right. In fact she never let any holiday pass without some semblance of tradition.

In March, given that her maiden name was Brennan, she always made sure to drag him off to an Irish pub, drink green beer, and sing folk songs all night. In April, there was a spiral cut, honey-baked ham, and their two daughters would be home for Easter. June 15th, their anniversary, was always spent at a bed & breakfast somewhere. It was a new one every year. It didn't matter what bed & breakfast it was, just that it was a B&B on their special day.

July 4th — the fireworks at the county fair. Halloween was always done up big, with gravestones in the front yard, ghosts hanging from the trees, a big cauldron with dry ice on the front porch, and lots of candy for the neighborhood kids. Cheri had kind words for each of the kids' costumes who came to trick or treat. Thanksgiving was a quiet affair, with the girls home again, and turkey with all the fixings. But Black Friday was anything but, in their house. It was always red, green, and white Friday, because Cheri always woke early and began preparing for Christmas, her absolute favorite holiday.

Ellis smiled, thinking about it. Cheri would begin playing Christmas music as soon as she awoke, and then put him to work; dragging out the decorations, making sure the lights worked and hanging them on the house, then setting up the Christmas tree. That night, after turkey sandwiches, and apple pie, she would make hot buttered rum from a recipe she got out of an old dilapidated Dickensian cookbook she found at a garage sale, and they would decorate the tree. Afterward they would step back, admire their work, take each other in their arms, and dance to the Christmas music until they were too tired to stay awake.

If he was forced to choose one specific day out of the year as his favorite, Ellis would have to say Black Friday.

But it wasn't just that day that was special at Christmastime. The first Saturday of December was practically a holiday unto itself. Cheri worked all day making hors d'oeuvres for the huge "Kick-off Christmas" party she threw for all of their family and friends. Their house would be packed with people from the neighborhood, from her office with her job at the state, from his division office at the airport, and even friends they met through the kids' school. Everyone was welcome, and they all came to see Cheri, and just spend a few minutes with her warm, special energy. It seemed to Ellis that Cheri had a bright, enlightening smile on her face, from Thanksgiving to New Year's Day.

Feeling a tickle on his cheek, he wiped at it, surprised to find it was a tear. He wiped the moisture around in his fingertips. When would the sadness end? When was he supposed to stop missing her?

Strawberry meowed quietly and nudged at his belly with her head. She wanted his hand back where it belonged — petting her. Ellis scratched behind her ears and looked around the cold, stark living room, dimming now as the light of day waned.

In his heart he knew that Cheri would be disappointed in him. It was December 23rd, and he hadn't bothered to get out one single decoration. He couldn't bring himself to do it. Black Friday was now his least favorite day of the year. And he'd even kept the radio off since Thanksgiving because he couldn't bear to hear the Christmas carols.

The phone on the table next to him started playing "Butterfly Kisses." Cheri had set that song up as a ring tone for him so he'd know when one of his daughters was calling. He never told her he hated the song. "Sorry, Strawberry, I have to take this." It was Kate, their oldest, making a video call from Seattle. He clicked the button and held it in front of him. "Hi, Sweetheart."

She had her mother's bright smile. "Hey there, Dad. What're you doing?"

"Oh, I'm just sitting here with Strawberry and Rhubarb," he angled the phone down so she could see the cat on his lap. "Relaxing and watching the dust settle."

"Hi, Strawberry," Kate sounded like she was talking to a two-month-old baby.

The only reaction Strawberry had was to nuzzle at the hand that should be scratching her ears.

Ellis chuckled and looked back into the phone. "She's got about as much energy as I do right now."

Kate tilted her head, furrowed her brow and tsked. "Dad, don't you have any plans? Aren't you going to have people over or something?"

"Oh, no." Ellis shook his head. "That was your mother's thing. Not mine. I wouldn't even know how to get ready for something like that, let alone want to have to deal with anyone right now."

"Beer and pizza." Kate rolled her eyes. "You know how to get beer and pizza. Anybody will come over for that."

"Kate, I don't want them over."

"Dad, you can't just…"

"Kate." Ellis wasn't much in the mood to hear the speech again. "I've told you. These are the last firsts. I just have to get through them the best way possible."

"You could still come out here you know. Cassie is coming up from Sacramento tomorrow, and she's going to stay for a few days. You can join us. We'd love to spend the time with you."

Ellis sighed. She had a point. She'd been inviting him every week since before Thanksgiving. He'd almost taken her up on it a couple of times, thinking a change of scenery might just be the trick. In fact, he'd considered driving the whole way from Iowa to Washington with Strawberry and Rhubarb in tow. But something had stopped him every time. Like he wasn't supposed to leave. He didn't want to run away from Cheri's memory, but sitting and facing it was almost too much to bear. He was a complete mess of a human being and he knew it. And even though he knew his daughters were worried about him, he wasn't ready to give them what they needed either.

"Kate, I love you. And I appreciate your invitation …again. But the best way for me to get through this is to ignore the fact that it's Christmas. I've been doing pretty well so far. I've just got a few more days to go and then it's done."

"Dad, it breaks my heart to see you wishing your days away."

"I'm not wishing all of them away, Sweetie. Just the good ones."

Kate's face grew large in the screen. "I love you, Dad."

"I love you too, Katydid. Tell that fiancé of yours I said hi, and tell Cassie I love her too." Ellis clicked off the call just as his vision blurred with tears. He dabbed at them with his shirt sleeve and sniffled.

The chimes of the doorbell jarred him. "What now?" He lifted Strawberry off his lap and set her back on the floor—not without protest. Then he dragged himself up from the chair.

When he opened the door he saw the cheery face of Ellen Mueller from across the street. She and her husband, Perry, had come to several of Ellis and Cheri's Christmas parties. Ellen was a short woman, light-gray hair. But what she lacked in stature she made up with in smile. "Hello, Ellis. I know you've been feeling a bit down this year. I saw you didn't even have your beautiful lights up. I'm sure it's probably very difficult and all, so I brought you over a plate of cookies. I thought someone should do something nice for you for a change."

Ellis looked down at the plate of cookies in her hands. Ellen Mueller's sugar cookies were renowned. Not only were they the most delicious sugar cookies on the planet, secret family recipe and all, but Ellen raised the bar in her decorations. Christmas trees with presents, shaded properly, intricate snowflakes. Each cookie was suitable for framing and placing on the wall.

But to Ellis they were repulsive. Just another thing to remind him that Christmas was here, and Cheri wasn't. "I don't know why everyone feels it's important to cheer me up. All I'm trying to do is forget about the holidays and everybody feels like it's their mission to make sure I don't. Did I ask you to come over and cheer me up?"

Ellen backed up a small step. "Well…uh…no…but…"

"So take the hint. I don't want your damn cookies, Ellen."

Ellen continued to stammer. "I…I'm…so sor…" The door slammed.

Ellis heard the voice of an old woman behind him, "How rude." He spun around only to find an empty room. "Hello?" He said. But nobody answered back. Strawberry and Rhubarb sat side by side, next to his chair staring at him. Ellis shook his head and scoffed. "I'm beginning to lose it. I need to finish this day in bed." He turned and walked across the room. "C'mon, Rhubarb. It's night-night time."

The old border collie lifted himself and pranced over to the sliding glass door like he had done every day for the last fourteen years, for Ellis to let him out to do his end-of-the-day-business.

"Operation Sleep-Through-the-Holidays begins now." Ellis went into the bathroom, took his prescription sleep aid, and got himself ready for bed.

He opened the sliding glass door one more time, and Rhubarb sauntered back in and climbed into his basket in the kitchen. Strawberry gave a goodnight meow and took her place under the couch. Ellis shuffled off to bed, read three pages from an old Tom Clancy novel until he couldn't keep his eyes open any longer, then closed the book, turned off the light and escaped into a lonely sleep once more.

* * *

Morning light streaming through the windows brought him out of his deep slumber. His eyes fluttered open to see Rhubarb lying in the bed next to him, head on his paws. When the dog noticed he was awake, he lifted his head and looked toward the back of the bed. Ellis followed the gaze to see Strawberry, sitting at the end of the bed, waiting.

Ellis rubbed the sleep out of his eyes, muttering, "What are you two doing here?"

Rhubarb's paw reached up and touched Ellis's arm. And with a low voice the dog spoke. "We're very worried about you, Ellis."

"What the...?" Ellis jerked away from Rhubarb.

The little border collie sat up and spoke again. "It's time we had a talk."

Ellis screamed, scampered away from the dog, falling out of bed with a large thunk, knocking over the nightstand in the process, bringing the clock, lamp, and glass of water crashing to the floor.

2

A rather high-pitched, older woman's voice cried out. "Are you all right?"

Ellis looked up from the mess to see Strawberry, on the edge of the bed, staring down at him. Her small whiskered mouth moved, and Ellis heard the voice again. "You're not hurt, are you?"

Ellis screamed once more, kicked and crawled away from the bed into the closet, knocking some of Cheri's gowns off their hangers, and sending them streaming down on his head.

"Please be careful," Strawberry said.

Frantic, Ellis struggled with the glittered garments, finding a hole he could stick his head through.

Rhubarb crawled across the bed to lie next to where Strawberry was sitting. He glanced over at the cat. "We were told this might be the reaction."

Ellis shook his head. "This isn't real. I'm still asleep." He pinched his skin. "Ouch." It left a red mark. He shouldn't have been so committed with his test.

"Please relax, Ellis," Strawberry said. "We just want to have a word with you."

"It's the pills," Ellis whispered. He looked over and saw the white prescription bottle lying on the floor next to the toppled nightstand. He pointed a finger at the animals. "Stay where you are." He crawled out slowly, one open palm facing them. "Stay. Just, stay."

With one powder blue and one red glittery gown draped over him, Ellis scurried on all fours to the bottle, snatched it up, then slid back to the far corner and clambered backward into the chair. "Let's see here." Ellis spun the little bottle around in his hands trying to locate the warning label and find out the side effects. "Where is it? What's it say?" Not seeing anything immediately on the outside of the bottle, he scratched at the flap of the label that opened up the more detailed instructions.

"Ellis, please let us talk to you," Rhubarb said again.

Ellis did not look up. He held up one hand. "Stop speaking." He located what he was looking for on the label. "Here it is. This is what you are." He held up the bottle and read it to the animals. "You are...daytime drowsiness, dizziness, weakness, loss of coordination, stuffy nose, nasal irritation, dry mouth, sore throat, nausea, constipation, diarrhea, upset stomach, headache, muscle pain, insomnia." He pulled the bottle down and vigorously nodded at them both. "That's what you are."

Rhubarb looked over at Strawberry. "I'm sure you're the constipation."

Strawberry scoffed and put a paw to her nose. "Speak for yourself, Mr. Nasal Irritation."

Ellis leaned forward, yelling at them. "Stop talking. *Now*."

"Oh, Ellis," Strawberry said. She hopped down from the bed and sat on the floor in front of him. "It's quite easy to get us to stop talking. All you have to do is listen for a moment."

"Listen?" Ellis said. "Listen to what?"

"Listen to those of us who love you." Rhubarb said. He perched tentatively on the edge of the bed, judging the distance to the floor, finally easing out and letting gravity bring his tired old body down. He sat next to Strawberry. "We're very worried about you. We want you to be okay, but you have to want that for yourself."

"I don't know what you're talking about. I *am* okay."

"Really?" Strawberry said. "I'm not sure poor old Mrs. Mueller would agree. She left here in tears. And all she did was try to do something nice for you. Do you think Cheri would approve of how you acted? Is this what you learned from her about the holidays? About life?"

Words stuck in Ellis's throat, like a log jam just behind his tongue. He tried to speak, but only strange guttural sounds came out.

"Even before yesterday," Rhubarb said. "You drag yourself off to work every morning, and drag yourself home even slower. You remember to give us food, but that is about all. I'm not sure I've had a walk with you in over a year. You let me out in the morning and at night, but that is the only fresh air I get. My old bones are getting weary."

Strawberry cleared her throat. "And I don't think Cheri would approve of how you have turned your back on your children."

"My children?" Ellis said. "My children understand I have to get through this year of firsts."

"Year of firsts." Strawberry looked over at Rhubarb. "How long have we been hearing that drivel?"

Rhubarb laid down with his head up. "About a year now."

"Yes." Strawberry scratched at her whiskers, then shook her head. "In two weeks and two days it will be one year. Are you telling me that on that magical day you will no longer miss Cheri, and you'll be able to move on with your life as though she never existed?"

"Well...no..."

"Of course not. You will still miss her. And so will we."

Ellis was surprised. "You miss her too?"

Rhubarb scoffed. "Oh boy, do we ever miss her. But we miss you too."

"All right. That's enough," Ellis said. "Yes, I've been sad. I was married to the sweetest, kindest, most giving, and most beautiful woman I've ever known, or ever will know. She was what gave me my energy to live—to get out of bed each day and attack the world. Without her, life is *not* the same. I'm just trying to cope with that."

"Are you listening to yourself, Ellis?" Strawberry said. "You act like life, from here to forever, will not be any good any longer. It's like you've made that decision, without ever giving life a chance to prove you wrong. But let me ask you this. If Cheri was such a bright light in your dark world, how are you honoring her life by wallowing the rest of yours away?"

"That's not a fair question."

"Isn't it?" Rhubarb said, lifting his head again. "How about this one then? You have two beautiful daughters and a great many friends, like Mrs. Mueller who love and care for you very much. Why don't you let them help you? Or even better, help *them* with something? By giving a little of yourself, you're honoring your late wife, whom you've already said was the most giving person you've ever known. Why don't you try to live like she did? Spread a little happiness in her memory."

"This is where you don't understand humans very well," Ellis said. "Humans are weighed down by emotion. You can't give of yourself when you're feeling hollow inside. You have to have something to give. I have to get through this year of firsts, then the healing can begin."

"I've got a newsflash for you, Mr. Higher-Life-Form." Rhubarb said. "I understand you better than you think. And I know this for a fact—even though you are sad and lost inside, you can still create happiness in others. And by making the decision to do so, you start to fill up your own emptiness. What *you* don't understand, Ellis, is there are a whole lot of people out there just like you, with heartaches and loneliness, especially at this time of the year. And they could use a guy like you, who had such an amazing role-model like Cheri, to spread a little warmth their way."

"Exactly," Strawberry said. "And wouldn't that be a much better way to remember her than hiding away from everything and everyone? You just said she was your energy to attack the world. Let her memory be that same energy."

Ellis laid his head back and looked up at the ceiling. He could feel the grief rise in him, saw the tears muddle his vision, then trickle down his cheeks.

Rhubarb stepped over, nuzzled at his calf, then put his paws on Ellis's knees. "I understand it's difficult, Ellis. But I also know that if you don't make an effort, you will never make it out of this hole you've fallen into. The year of firsts will become a year of seconds, and then a year of thirds. Cheri deserves more from you than that."

Ellis wiped at his eyes, then looked back down at his...pets. "I don't even know how to go about what you're asking me to do."

"We can help," Strawberry said. "Do you trust us?"

Ellis couldn't help but laugh at this question. "I'm sitting here having a heart-to-heart conversation with my cat and my dog. I don't even trust my own sanity right now."

Strawberry giggled. "Good point. Well, let me explain it to you. We animals have a little communication that we call...you don't have a word for it, so just think of it as our own type of Wi-Fi."

Ellis shrugged. "Okay. The 'inter-pet.'"

Rhubarb chuckled. "That was a good one."

Strawberry hopped up on Ellis's lap. "I'm going to send you along the...'inter-pet' and help you find others who need you, specifically."

"And how do you propose to do that?"

Strawberry positioned herself on his legs, raised up and put her front paws on his chest just below his neck. "Just look into my eyes, and don't fight it."

She was so close, Ellis couldn't focus on her eyes, but he looked into them anyway. Soon a strange glow appeared in the pupil of each cat eye. The light seemed to sap his strength. He quickly felt drowsy. In another second, consciousness left him, and all was dark.

3

The next thing Ellis noticed was the acrid smell of hay mixed with manure. He opened his eyes to see an old, gray wooden wall of a stall. *What did that cat do to me?*

Then the pain clenched tight in his gut. He reached down to clutch at his stomach, but his hands felt heavy, clumsy. They didn't work like they should. He cried out in pain and was surprised to hear a loud, angry neighing.

"There, there, boy. I know." A calm voice said. "It hurts like a sonuvagun."

What is going on here? Ellis wanted to say, but it came out in grunts and gurgles.

He lifted his heavy head, and noticed his large snout. A man, with glasses, jeans and a bright green rubber jacket was leaning over him, hand on Ellis's neck, rubbing gently.

It was beginning to dawn on Ellis, what was happening. *The cat turned me into a horse.* He sniffled and snorted, then cried out again, trying to ask what was going on. The neighing seemed frantic, and the man straightened and stood back.

"Easy, Mr. Smith," he said. Ellis tried to stand, but the pain in his gut pulled him right back down.

"Doc. What's going on?"

Tilting his head, Ellis now noticed two more men standing behind the man in the green rubber jacket. The one who just spoke was older. He had a cowboy hat, with gray hair curling out from under it. His shirt was tucked in tightly, with his belly protruding out over the waist of his blue jeans. He wore a brown corduroy jacket, and he was draped over the end of the stable wall, like a rag doll hung on a nail.

The man in the green rubber jacket turned to him and shook his head. "I've given him three shots of pain killers and it doesn't seem to be touching the pain. He can't even stand now, which is not a good sign at all. He's been colicking all night." He pointed to the ground in front of Ellis. "He'd been pawing for quite some time. He practically dug a trench right here in the stable. That would have been the time to do something. Even if you'd have given him water then, it might have helped some."

Wait. Colicking? That's just gas, right? Give me a couple of horse-sized Rolaids. That's all you have to do, right?

"What are you saying?" The old man's voice quivered slightly.

The pain intensified in Ellis's gut. He lurched, and cried out once more.

"His gut flipped and his intestines are all wound up. I think necrosis has set in, and his organs are starting to shut down."

I'm dying? Strawberry and Rhubarb turned me into a dying horse? Why would they do this to me?

"Oh, God," The man on the other side of the stall said. He was younger, dirty, red down jacket unzipped, showing a Brad Paisley t-shirt underneath. Both hands were on his head, pushing down his shoulder-length blond hair. He turned to the old man. "Mr. Kobbs, I'm so sorry."

"I don't want to hear it." Old man Kobbs stood straight. The younger man stepped back. "I hired you to take care of the animals, and you do this." Kobbs gestured toward Ellis.

Another pain seared through his gut, and Ellis let out his loudest neigh yet. He tried to scoot and stretch to help ease the pain, find some comfort, but it helped very little.

"But Mr. Kobbs, it's Christmas tomorrow. I had things I had to take care of."

"Oh, were you still planning on taking your paycheck, even though you didn't check on any of the animals yesterday?"

"Mr. Kobbs, I did..."

"Enough, Brookes!" Kobbs took another step forward. The young man stepped back again. Kobbs pointed at Ellis. "Tell Mr. Smith it's Christmas. See if that matters at all to him."

The young man named Brookes looked back down at Ellis, who was apparently named Mr. Smith.

"Better yet, just get the hell off my land, Brookes. Don't let me ever see you around here again."

Brookes scoffed, dropped his shoulders, and stomped out of the barn.

Ellis twisted and whinnied once more. The pain was traumatizing, and try as he might, he could not find a comfortable position.

Kobbs dropped to his knees and stroked Ellis's head. "I'm so sorry, Mr. Smith." Ellis could see tears in the old man's eyes now. "Give us a minute, boy. We're going to make the pain go away." He turned to the man in the green rubber jacket. "Okay, Doc. Let's take care of him."

Doc nodded solemnly, then stepped out of view.

Take care of me...what does that mean? They shoot horses, don't they? Are you going to kill me?

Pain cut at his mid-section once more, and Ellis made the horse-equivalent of doubling over, his pained whinnying as loud as ever. *Okay, I can't take this any longer. Please kill me.*

Kobbs sat on the hay, and pulled Ellis/Mr. Smith's head onto his lap. The old man was crying now. He rubbed at his tears and his nose with the sleeve of his corduroy jacket, and patted his horse's snout. "It's okay, boy. I know it hurts. We're going to help you now."

It felt like a knife entered Ellis's abdomen, and he had to shift, and kick once more. He hoped they'd get on with it.

Doc stepped into view carefully holding a large syringe with a long needle.

"I need you to hold his head firmly," Doc said. "I don't want him jerking and breaking the needle off in his neck."

Kobbs braced himself with his back against the wall of the stable. Ellis could feel the old man wrap one leg over his neck and hold his head tightly with both hands.

Out of the corner of his eye, Ellis could see Doc lean in and then felt a slight pinch. "Okay, boy," Doc said, patting his neck. "It won't hurt much longer."

"Rest now, Mr. Smith," Kobbs said. The old man shook with grief.

A warmth coursed through Ellis's...no...Mr. Smith's body. The pain receded, like a wave sliding away from the shore. Every muscle in his large, strong frame was able to relax. And Mr. Smith could finally take an easy breath. Extreme weariness set in, and Mr. Smith's eyes began to flutter.

What is going to happen to me? Am I done too, along with Mr. Smith? Did my own cat kill me by pulling this crazy stunt?

His horse eyes closed and remained that way, no longer having the strength to even lift his eyelids. Kobbs's words and weeping became distant and soft, until Ellis could no longer hear them again. All he could hear was the slow labored breathing of the horse—a rhythm that grew slower with each heavy, ragged breath.

Then the breathing stopped.

4

Ellis heard his own scream from the distant darkness—quiet at first, but growing closer and louder, until his eyes popped open, and he lurched forward. He was drenched with sweat and panting wildly.

Strawberry and Rhubarb were lying on the floor in front of him. They both raised their heads.

"What the hell was that?" He screamed.

"That was your first animal lesson," Strawberry said. "How was it?"

Ellis jumped to his feet. "It hurt!" He stomped into the bathroom, turned on the water in the sink, and splashed his face.

The cat and the dog dragged themselves in after him. "So what did you learn from the experience?"

"Learn?" Ellis grabbed a towel and dabbed at his face. "What was I supposed to learn from inside a dying horse? I suppose I learned that colic in a horse hurts like hell." He wiped the back of his neck and threw the towel in the hamper.

"So Mr. Smith died?" Rhubarb shook his head and lay back down. "That's sad."

"It happens." Ellis shrugged. "Especially to horses."

"How rude," Strawberry said. "I would think you'd have a little more compassion."

"How did you even do that anyway?" Ellis walked back to the chair and slumped into it.

"The how isn't as important as the why," Rhubarb said. "You were supposed to meet Mr. Kobbs and see how sad he is too."

"Yea, he was sad. But he only lost a horse." Ellis sat back up. "Are you comparing him losing a horse, to me losing the love of my life?"

"No," Rhubarb said.

"Good. Because there's no comparison."

Strawberry jumped up on the arm of the chair. "Mr. Randal Kobbs isn't sad because he lost Mr. Smith. He's sad because his grandson was killed last June. He was hit by a car, while riding his bike. The driver was a teenager who had been texting."

Ellis thought for a moment, contemplating Mr. Kobbs's reaction. "Then why did he cry so much for Mr. Smith?"

"Mr. Smith was his grandson's horse. It was all the man had left of the boy."

"Well, what about Mrs. Kobbs?"

"In a care facility," Rhubarb said. "She has Alzheimer's. She can't be at home any longer, and she really isn't that coherent anymore, anyway."

"Okay," Ellis said. "His kids?"

"He has one son," Strawberry said. "He lives somewhere in Georgia. He is also consumed with grief as you might imagine, and won't be home for Christmas."

Ellis sat back and rubbed at his chin. "Huh."

"You see, Ellis," Rhubarb said. "You aren't the only one sad on Christmas Eve."

"Exactly." Strawberry jumped down and stood next to her canine friend. "What would Cheri say about Mr. Kobbs, knowing he was alone at this time of year?"

Ellis frowned. "Wait a minute. I see what you're doing. You're telling me stories to make me feel guilty. How would you even know any of that anyway?"

"Through the inter-pet," Strawberry said.

Ellis shook his head. "The inter-pet?"

"Well you named it," Strawberry said. "And I think the word works rather nicely."

"Well, I don't buy it."

"Then it's time for your next journey," Rhubarb said.

"Oh, no." Ellis sat back and held his hands out in front of him. "Stay away from me. I'm not doing that again."

"We don't have to get near you," Rhubarb said. "You never got off the line. It's a good thing you're sitting down."

Ellis's arms felt instantly heavy, and they dropped down on either side of the chair. His eyelids drooped, then closed, and consciousness quickly slid away.

5

Though he tried to shout the words, "Not again," what Ellis heard was a sharp, "BahAhAhAhAh." His head spun, and he lost his footing from the rather soft lump he'd been standing on. He fell sideways, hearing gasps on his way to colliding with a hard wooden floor.

"Oh, poor thing." A young woman said.

"BahAhAhAhAh," He said, and clambered to his feet—all four of them. His eyes fluttered, and came into focus. He now stood in a large, dim, wooden building. The floor was wooden planks; old, but clean. Five women in yoga pants and t-shirts, two of which had no business being in yoga pants, crouched on colorful mats on the floor. They all looked at him with concern.

You've got to be kidding me. The cat has turned me into a pygmy goat? Am I in a goat yoga class?

At least he wasn't in any pain this time. But he was a bit hungry.

"Are you okay, Deepak?" Another woman said from behind him.

Ellis turned to see one lone woman on a bright green mat in the front of the room. She was on all fours and staring at him. "Deepak?" She said. "Are you okay, buddy?"

"BahAhAhAhAh," Ellis said again, without realizing it. He walked toward the woman and his feet—no, hooves, clunked on the floorboards. The woman looked Latino, and her long dark hair, streaked with gray, was pulled back in a ponytail. She wore no make-up, and he could see crow's feet creeping out from the edges of her eyes.

What he noticed next was the bright green of the mat she was crouched on. It looked delicious somehow. He stepped up, brought his little bearded chin down to the mat, and started to nibble at the corner.

"Deepak, stop that." The woman pushed him away, and giggled. "This is a brand new mat, and it's my Christmas present to myself. I'd like to at least have it kept nice for one day before you eat *it* up too."

There were giggles from the other woman as well. "Falling didn't hurt his appetite any." One of them said.

"BahAhAhAhAh," Ellis said.

The small group of women laughed again.

"Okay, let's finish this up now," The woman on the green mat spun her legs around and sat facing the class.

"We'll lie back and do one last easy stretch." She lay on her back, with her arms over her head. The five women followed her instruction. "Fingers and toes as far away from each other as your body will possibly allow, and stretch."

Ellis continued to look around, fascinated by this place. Ethereal-sounding music came from speakers at every corner. Lit candles were set in mason jars around the perimeter of the room, and small white Christmas lights draped down from the plank ceiling.

"Okay, now put your hands by your side. Time to relax. Use these last few minutes to rest your mind and recharge. You need to prepare yourself before the holiday activities."

A small desk with a computer and a tall, old-style, black file cabinet was positioned next to the entrance. At the front of the room, a large sign hung above the woman running the class. It started with the letters, "Sh," and ended with the word "Barn." A large green plastic banner covered it, decorated with snowflakes which said "Happy Holidays" in red letters. Another sign underneath it had the word "Namaste" in big, pastel green letters.

The place was incredibly peaceful and Ellis was afraid to move even the slightest, for fear he would disturb the meditation of these women.

But the opening of the front door interrupted the tranquility. A tall man entered. He removed his long, dark, winter coat and hung it on a rack, exposing his bulging chest. He wore a gold and black sweater, black denims, dark boots. He had short cut hair, military-style, to match his military physique. Crossing his arms, he leaned his back against the wall, and smiled at the woman in front.

Ellis looked at her. She looked back at the man, smile clearly absent, then laid her head back down and closed her eyes.

For several more minutes the women lay there, listening to the wisps of music that filled the air and calmed their spirits. The man in the corner remained motionless at the doorway, waiting patiently.

Finally the woman sat up and spoke softly, "Okay, come back now. You are ready to face the holidays, and all of the challenges and the stresses that come with them."

The women opened their eyes, and slowly sat up. Some yawned, some stretched, all looked weary.

The class leader stood and clapped her hands. "All right, let's go and have a great Christmas. You got this!"

The women rolled up their mats and climbed to their feet. "Thanks so much for this class, Julia," one of the women said, and hugged the instructor. Others followed suit and wished her Merry Christmas. Some of them looked at the man at the door, turned to her with a smile, and winked. The woman named Julia awkwardly smiled back.

They gathered their coats and belongings, wished the man at the doorway a Merry Christmas, and exited the building.

When the door had closed on the last woman, Julia spoke up. "What are you doing here, Brad?"

Brad gave her his killer smile. His cheeks dimpled up. "Hello to you too, Julia. You look great as well."

Julia scoffed. "Of course you look great, Brad. You always have, and you know it."

Brad stepped away from the wall. "Thank you. You're as beautiful as ever. Yoga pants are a good look for you. They show all the right curves."

Julia scoffed again, walked over and pulled a large bag out of the bottom drawer of the old black file cabinet. She turned to Ellis, eyebrows raised. "Deepak, are you all right, buddy? You've never just watched me grab your chaffhaye, and not jumped all over me."

Because I have no idea what the hell that is.

Ellis clunked across the floor toward her. Julia leaned down and poured the contents of the bag into a plastic bin next to the cabinet. The chaffhaye looked like something Ellis blew off the driveway after he was done mowing. But the smell drove him crazy for some reason. Once the sweet and tangy aroma hit his nostrils, he couldn't get his face into the bin fast enough. The taste was even more remarkable. It was tart, fermented, with just the right crunch in his mouth.

Oh my gosh, I'm like a pygmy goat foodie.

"Did the goat come with the barn?" Brad said, smirking.

"And there it is," Julia said.

"There what is?"

Julia crossed her arms and sat on the edge of the little desk. "That thing where you disapprove of everything I do."

Brad chuckled. "Hey. C'mon now. I'm only kidding." He walked over and put his hands on her shoulders. "I'm not disapproving. I'm in awe of this place. You've done a lot with yourself in the last year."

"Yes, I have. And I'm proud of myself. I bought this barn and fixed it up with the money Dad left me, and my business is really starting to take off."

Ellis/Deepak munched away at his special treat, looking up occasionally to watch the drama unfold.

Brad stepped back. "You spent the entire inheritance from your dad on this place?"

Julia stood. "Well the entire inheritance didn't cover all of the refitting needed, so I took out a small business loan too." She walked around the room and blew out the candles in the jars along the walls.

Brad put his hands on his hips. "That's uhhh...I guess that's pretty...bold."

"Bold doesn't cover it." She blew into a jar extinguishing the candle then set it back on the floor. "I've got balls bigger than any man I know. And it's paying off too." She gestured to the room. "Those women *requested* today's class. Practically begged me. I wasn't even going to be open on Christmas Eve, but they all said they'd pay me double if I'd help them center themselves before their families arrived."

"That's fantastic, Julia," Brad said. "But don't you think it was maybe just a slight bit...reckless?"

"You know another 'r'-word that's worse than 'reckless,' Brad? 'Regret.'" She blew out another candle and pointed the jar at him. "And that is something I've decided to keep out of my life."

Brad walked into the center of the room. "Then let me congratulate you on all of your success, Julia. I truly am happy for you. But now comes the million dollar question. What about us? Where do we go from here?"

Julia shrugged. "What are you talking about? We broke up."

"No. We separated. I said I would give you a year to figure things out."

"Yes. *You* said a year. I never said a year. And now you show up here, on Christmas Eve, to do this."

Brad put his hands on his hips again. "I'm back on Christmas Eve, because we parted on Christmas Eve last year." He pointed at her. "And I want you to know it was probably the worst Christmas of my life."

"What am I supposed to do with that information, Brad?" Julia slammed the jar back down on the floor. "It was *probably* the worst Christmas of your life?" She stood and looked at him. "I would think that if you were really trying to get me back, it would have *definitely* been the worst Christmas of your life."

"There you go again, with all your semantics."

Julia crossed her arms and bit at her lower lip. "Look," She walked over to face Brad. "I'm not doing this. And it's not because you're a selfish asshole. It's because I don't do pairs well. I never have, and I realize I never will. Just accepting that fact has turned my life around and made me stronger."

"What are you saying, Julia?"

"I'm saying it's not you, it's me."

Brad stood straighter. "Are you telling me I waited a year of my life for nothing?" He puffed his chest out. "I lost an entire year, waiting for a selfish bitch?"

Ellis didn't like the way this was sounding. Though he hated to do it, he turned away from his bowl and stepped toward them. "BahAhAhAhAh."

That didn't sound as menacing as I'd hoped.

Brad glanced over at him and scowled.

At least I got his attention.

Brad looked back at her, his body as tense as a coiled spring. "Fine. Let your damn goat keep you warm on cold winter nights." He stomped over, yanked his coat off the hook and turned back to her. "And just for the record, it *was* the worst Christmas of my life. So you are turning your back on a man who loved you. Hey, wait. Now you have to live with a regret. You poor, sad thing." He slammed the door open and stormed out of the barn.

Julia exhaled, releasing the stress and tension she had been hiding since the moment he walked into the room.

Ellis walked over to her.

She knelt down and hugged him. "Thanks, buddy. I don't know what would've happened if you hadn't spoken up when you did." With a sad smile, Julia stood and continued extinguishing the candles.

Ellis walked back and shoved his head into the bin for another mouthful of the marvelous feed.

When the candles were out, Julia went to her desk, turned off the lamp, and shut down her computer. The ethereal music fell silent. "Come on, Deepak. It's time to take your dinner upstairs."

Ellis/Deepak felt a surge of panic when Julia grabbed his bin of feed and walked away. Still chewing and grunting, he was right at her heels, waiting for the moment she would put it back down, and he could grab another mouthful.

Rounding a corner, Julia ascended a set of dark wooden stairs that led to a closed door at the top.

Ellis watched her go up, saw bright light at the top when the door opened. Julia stepped into the well-lit room and looked back down at him. "What's wrong, buddy? Please tell me you're not feeling sick."

Ellis swallowed his lump of feed and spoke to reassure her that he was doing just fine. "BahAhAhAhAh." He took a few cautious steps, never having climbed stairs with four legs before. He quickly found out how natural the process felt.

That's right. Goats can walk on pebbles on the side of cliffs.

Bounding up the rest of the way, he landed next to her on the stoop of a very comfortable-looking studio apartment. The floor was the same old wooden beams which were the planked ceiling down below. Large colorful area rugs were strewn about the room. The old barn boards were covered with drywall and painted a bright white. Mixed media paintings, pastel drawings, and fluffy cloth art covered the walls. A modest kitchen with a large island stood at the top of the stairs. A flat screen TV was mounted to the opposite wall, with a cozy-looking blue cloth-covered sofa in front of it. Her apartment was one of the brightest, cheeriest places he had ever seen.

Julia set his bin of goodness next to the island and walked into a small room off the kitchen. Ellis shoved his face back into the bowl when he heard her call out, "Dammit!" Mouth crunching away, he peered around the edge of the island to see Julia stomp out of the room, and look back into it, lips curled into an angry snarl. She stood there for a moment, her hands on her hips, sighing in frustration, before she shook her head and muttered, "To hell with it." She strode past him, out the door and down the stairs.

Ellis wondered what had gotten her so upset, and he was going to check, once he licked the remainder of the chaffhaye out of the bin.

A few moments later he heard a toilet flush from below him. Footsteps rushed up the stairs, and through the door breezed Julia, a plunger in hand. She rushed into the next room, and Ellis could hear the familiar sounds of a toilet being plunged.

The bin slid across the floor as he licked it, coming to rest when it bumped into the sofa. This gave him the opportunity to make sure there were no yummy bits left along the sides.

With the ambiance of sloshing water and four-letter words, Ellis/Deepak decided to wander around the little apartment to figure out what Julia's story was. Pictures on a table under the TV showed images of a smiling younger Julia with a gray-haired white man in front of the Statue of Liberty and in Times Square. Ellis assumed the man was her father. Other pictures showed her with a Latina woman, he was sure was her mother, in front of Mt. Rushmore, and one with the three of them in front of the Corn Palace, an Iowa staple.

Finally the toilet flushed. Ellis heard the sound of the sink running and soapy hands being squished together. In another moment, Julia emerged, sniffling, and wiping her eyes and nose with the palms of her hands. She went directly to the kitchen, pulled out a big kettle and dumped oil into it. As it warmed on the stove she grabbed a remote and clicked to a cheesy Christmas movie on the Hallmark Channel. She dumped an overflowing cup of popcorn into the oil, and soon the entire apartment smelled like a movie theater lobby. Julia popped up a huge bowl of popcorn, melted butter in the microwave and poured it over the top. She shook the bowl, salted it, and walked it over to the sofa.

There was a paper plate on the table that she placed several handfuls onto, then set the plate on the floor. "There's your share, Deepak. Let me know when you need more."

Ellis/Deepak couldn't help himself. The smell drove him crazy, and he had to have some popcorn.

Are goats just perpetually hungry? And everything looks delicious for some reason. This is ridiculous. How does little Deepak not weigh six hundred pounds?

Ellis turned his tail when Julia stripped out of her yoga clothes and into baggy sweats. She slipped on a pair of fluffy pink socks, strolled into the kitchen and pulled a beer out of the fridge, then plopped down on the couch in front of the Hallmark movie, grabbed her bowl of popcorn and munched away.

After a few moments she grabbed her phone and began tapping away at the screen.

I just don't know what more I'm supposed to see here. She's chosen to be alone on Christmas Eve.

He looked up at her, staring intently at her phone. The expressions on her face morphed from, frustration, to adoration. He wished he could just ask her. "BahAhAhAhAh," came out of his mouth once more, without even realizing it.

She smiled at him. "Since when do you ask my permission?" She patted the couch next to her. "Get up here, buddy."

He didn't need to be told twice. Ellis/Deepak hopped up and sat next to her. He was able to get a glimpse of her phone now. She was scrolling through Facebook, liking everything with hearts, and offering up a multitude of cheery holiday comments. After a while she put her phone down and grabbed her bowl of popcorn, turning her attention to the movie once more. Every now and then she would set a few pieces on the sofa for Ellis/Deepak and he would lap them up instantly.

The movie followed the typical format. Boy and girl meet at Christmastime. They don't get along. Circumstances throw them together to solve a problem. They discover they work very well together. They kiss on Christmas Day and live happily ever after. Julia dripped with tears. She ran to the bathroom to blow her nose, then to the kitchen for another beer, and was back in her seat just as the next movie came on.

Okay, guys. I'm done with this.

Nothing. He was still a goat.

He shook his head and lay down on the couch facing his head to the TV. If he was going to be stuck there, he might as well be comfortable. It wasn't long before his little goat eyes closed, and he drifted off to sleep.

6

Ellis awoke, still slouched in his chair. Strawberry and Rhubarb were nowhere in sight. He sat up to find the room was spinning slightly. He rubbed at his eyes, shook his head, and called out for his pets. "Hey. Where are you?"

"Well, you finally came back," Rhubarb said, strolling back into the room.

"It's about time," Strawberry said, bounding in behind him. "You've been gone for hours."

"Don't blame me. That was your doing."

"Yes, and no," Strawberry said.

"We can discuss that later. You've neglected us all day," Rhubarb said. "I need to go outside, and I'm hungry."

Ellis's stomach let out a low groan. "Oh my gosh, I'm hungry too. But I don't know how that can be, I've been eating all day."

"No you haven't," the cat said. "You been sitting there sleeping."

Ellis stood on wobbly legs, paused to get his balance, then walked out of the room. He opened the sliding glass door to the back yard.

Rhubarb let out a relieved sigh. "Thank you." The old border collie strode out the door.

Strawberry hopped up on the arm of the easy chair and tsked. "It's too bad dogs can't be more self-sufficient, don't you think?"

"Never mind that," Ellis said. "What was the big idea of sending me off to be a goat for a day?"

"Ah, yes. How was little Deepak, anyway?"

"Little Deepak was fine. Constantly hungry, but fine. I just don't know what the point of turning me into a goat was."

"It's not the animal, silly. It's the human that the animal cohabitates with, that's important."

"She was fine too. Once Brad Ass-hat left, that is."

A scratch was heard at the door behind him, and Ellis turned to see Rhubarb, ready to come back in. He slid open the door, and the old dog entered. "Okay, how about some dinner?"

"Dinner?" Ellis said, closing the door. "I haven't had breakfast yet." He walked into the kitchen, pulled a bag of dog food out of the pantry and poured it into the dish by the side of the refrigerator.

"Thanks again." Rhubarb stuck his head in the bowl and immediately crunched away.

Ellis watched him, surprised that now he knew exactly how grateful the little dog felt. "But that brings up a point." Ellis grabbed a bowl, spoon, box of Raisin Bran and the milk out of the fridge and took it to the table. "This Julia has never been married, so she doesn't understand the loss of someone she loved, like me or the old man does." He poured his Raisin Bran into the bowl. "And she is now choosing to live alone. So you basically wasted my time all day."

Rhubarb swallowed and turned to Strawberry. "I told you he wouldn't get it."

"I know you did," Strawberry said. "I'm sorry to say you were right."

"Because you hate it when I'm right."

"Yes. There is that. But I'm also sorry he's so thick in the head."

"Hey," Ellis said, pouring the milk. "I'm right here. Show a little respect." He shoveled a large scoop of cereal into his mouth.

"Ellis, this isn't about a competition of who is sadder on Christmas. The woman is lonely."

Ellis swallowed and looked over at the dog. "You're making less sense. I'm supposed to feel sorry for someone who's alone on Christmas because she *wants* to be."

"Oh, Ellis. Where is your compassion?" Strawberry hopped down from the easy chair and jumped up on the kitchen chair next to him. "Just because she made a choice *not* to be in a relationship doesn't mean she doesn't get lonely—especially during the holidays."

Ellis swallowed another mouthful and scoffed. "My heart isn't breaking for a woman, who doesn't want anybody around. Her loneliness is a product of her own choices."

Rhubarb sighed and walked over. "Okay, cat. I think it's monkey time."

Strawberry looked down at him and nodded. "It's looks like you're right again."

"Monkey time?" Ellis said. "You want to turn me into a monkey now? No thank you. Who has a monkey as a pet anyway?" He stuffed another spoonful into his mouth.

"You need to swallow that, Ellis," Strawberry said. "I don't want you to choke."

Ellis shook his head and raised his hand to stop the cat. "Uh-uh. No." He swallowed. "Enough of this…" His arms went limp, his eyes rolled up, and his eyelids closed. In the distance he could hear the spoon clatter to the floor.

7

There was a sudden sense of falling, like one gets when one is asleep and they jerk themselves awake.

Ellis jerked, and cried out. The sound surprised him. It was somewhere between a chirp and a grunt.

Two hands caught him and lifted him up. "Uko salama, Tumbili?"

Ellis looked into the face of a very small, African American man. He was gaunt, prematurely balding, and wearing big, baggy blue coveralls, with the sleeves and the pant-legs rolled up comically.

Oh my gosh. Where did those two send me now? Am I even still in the country?

The man lifted Ellis back onto his shoulder. Ellis clutched the man's collar with his *four?* fingers, and wrapped his *tail?* around the man's neck to balance.

The man reached up and adjusted, Ellis's tail, loosening it slightly. "Rahisi, Tumbili. Ninapumua." Then the man chuckled, and walked down a long, cement-block hallway. It was tinted yellow, under glowing halogen lights that buzzed overhead. The floor puddled in spots, and there was a lingering smell of waste in the air.

Am I in a prison somewhere? Is this like the monkey-man of Alcatraz or something?

Ellis examined himself. He was covered in grayish-brown fur. His toes and fingers were small and dark—and he confirmed, there were no thumbs on either hand. His tail, however, was long and strong.

I am definitely a little monkey, but I have no idea what kind. Nor do I know what I'm doing here.

They came to a small door with a sign that read "Clinic."

The sign is in English. At least I might still be in the USA.

The man pulled out keys and opened the door.

Once inside he lifted Ellis off his shoulder and set him down on a medical table. A short screech came out of Ellis's monkey-mouth, but then he sat quietly and watched.

The man swung open the squeaky beaten door of a large black cabinet, and pulled out a long metal rod, and a small black kit. He walked over and used his keys to open a smaller locked cabinet. From there he grabbed a vial and a clear plastic package that contained a large syringe with a long needle.

Ellis scratched at his belly and watched as the odd-looking man deftly assembled the needle, filled the syringe with the liquid from the vial, and attached it to the end of the metal rod which was obviously designed for this purpose.

"Njoo, Tumbili." The man reached down, lifted Ellis by the tail, and swung him back up on his shoulder. The man was obviously comfortable around monkeys...and syringes at the end of long metal rods.

The man grabbed the black kit and they left the room, heading back the way they'd come. Several yellow metal doors were spaced along the hallway. The man selected one, twisted the handle, it stuck. He kicked at it, and it swung open. They entered and the heavy door closed behind them automatically with a loud thunk.

Inside the musty room was a large metal cage attached to the cement wall, with a small slide door inside, and a large metal gate on the side. Opposite the cage was a big deep freeze. The man set the syringe rod and the black kit carefully on a chair. He opened the deep freeze, which turned out to be just a large, horizontal refrigerator. Inside was a big bag of bloody meat. He opened the bag, releasing a horrible stench, and pulled out a dripping red hunk the size of a human head. He let the lid of the fridge slam shut, opened the gate, and dropped the meat in with a splat, onto the cement floor. He wiped his bloody hands on his trousers, grabbed Ellis's tail, swung him over to the top of the fridge, and held his hand up. "Kaa, Tumbili. Kaa."

Ellis understood that "kaa" meant to stay put, and he could tell by now that his name was Tumbili.

The man walked across the room, grabbed a lever that stuck out from the wall, and pulled it down. The metal door slid open, and in rushed a very large tiger, heading right toward Ellis.

Instinctively screeching loudly, Ellis jumped back to the wall.

The tiger stood in the cage, his gaze drifted down to the meat, and back up to Ellis. His face twisted into a snarl and it growled, though Ellis could make out spoken words from the noise in a low, growly, feminine voice. "You come to me in angst. Do you expect me to feel sorry for you?"

Ellis's monkey breath caught in his monkey throat. *Who is she talking to? Does she know I'm not the monkey?*

The tiger continued to growl. "We have all lost someone we love. You aren't the only one who feels grief. But the strong are those who realize what they do have, and push on. You have the ability to roam free, to make your own choices."

Ellis's monkey body shivered from a chill that crept down its spine and along its long tail.

"But instead you choose to cage yourself, to bury your head, and grovel in sorrow." The tiger's growl became more intense. "You sicken me."

The tiger stopped growling, lowered her head, and tore at the meat with her massive teeth.

Ellis didn't know what to make of the tiger's words. Had the monkey lost someone as well? It was obvious the monkey had the chance to roam free. Perhaps that was the reason. Perhaps the monkey had lost someone, and this African man had taken pity on it, given it the option to live outside the cage while it grieved.

But the tone and the words struck at Ellis. He grew defensive and angry. Sure everybody loses someone they love, but Ellis had been married to Cheri longer than this tiger had even been alive, perhaps three times as long. So who did the tiger think she was to talk to Ellis like that? She had no idea what Ellis had lost, so she didn't even have the capacity to judge him. Ellis decided, whether the tiger was talking to him or the monkey, Ellis had a strong dislike for this creature.

Do you become a bigger asshole the higher you go on the food chain?

Holding the hunk of meat with her two front paws, the tiger ripped off a chunk, tipped her head back, and with quick jerks of her jaws, engulfed the treat.

The man backed up, slowly picked up the metal rod, and stepped to the cage, staying out of the tiger's eye line. When he was close enough, he slid the rod, syringe end first, through the cage, lowered it near the tiger's hind quarters, and with a quick thrust, jammed the needle deep, injecting the liquid.

With a snarl, the tiger spun around, but the man had already pulled the syringe rod out and was several steps away. With the tiger turned the other way, Ellis could then see bright red blood contrasted against the orange and black fur, running from a large gash on her neck.

The tiger turned several times in the tight confines of the little cage, then went back to the task of shredding and swallowing the meat. She lay down with her front paws holding the steak, while she ripped off small pieces. When she had downed the last of it, the tiger stood, licked her lips continuously and looked around for more. She then sat, licked at her paws, and blinked wearily. It wasn't long before she slid the rest of the way to the ground, and with a small yawn, lay on her side, and drifted off into unconsciousness.

As soon as the tiger's head touched the concrete, the man flipped the latch and opened the small gate. It squealed softly all the way open. The man crawled inside, dragging the black medical kit with him.

A nervous screech came out of the mouth of Ellis/Tumbili. It was so involuntary and foreign, the sound of his own voice made him jump.

The man looked up at Ellis and put a finger to his lips, then knelt next to the tiger and opened the kit. He pulled out a paper package, ripped it open, slid out the gauze and used it to pat at the tiger's wound. He opened a bottle of antiseptic, poured it on the cut and cleaned it. A low growl grumbled in the tiger's throat, loud enough to echo off the cement walls of the small room.

The man leaned over to check the tiger's eyes. They remained closed tightly. He turned, rummaged around in the bag, came out with a small kit containing a curved needle and thread. The man deftly threaded the needle, tied it off, turned back to the tiger. With slow, methodical precision, the man stitched together the massive gash in the tiger's neck.

The door to the room burst in, and Ellis/Tumbili let out another screech, and scurried to the corner of the fridge.

"Yeah, he's still in there!" It was a young security guard, red-haired, shirt untucked, talking on a cell phone that he held to his ear with his elbow high in the air.

Ellis could now tell where he was by the Billing Park Zoo patch on the guard's puffy winter coat.

"Kazi," The guard said to the small African man, "Ms. Rikter wants you out of there, *now*."

The commotion had not phased the man named Kazi. Keeping his attention on his task, he spoke with his thick African accent. "Almost finished. Will be out, very quickly."

"He says he's almost done," The guard said into the phone. Ellis could hear faint chatter from the phone's tiny speaker, then the guard looked back at Kazi. "She says you're finished now. You don't have clearance to be in there."

"Two more stitches," Kazi said.

"He's not coming out." The guard shifted his weight back and forth in the cramped quarters. "Okay." He pulled the phone down from his ear, hit the screen, and held it out toward Kazi. A woman's voice blared out; tinny. "Kazi, you're putting us in a very difficult situation here. If anything happened to you, provided you're still alive, not only would you be deported, but the zoo would be fined, lose its insurance, and quite possibly its license. I need you to get out of that cage now."

Kazi pulled the stitches tight and began to tie them off. "Kasool was severely cut in neck playing with Achilles. Bleeding bad. I do this very well."

The guard banged on the cage with his fist. "Dude, when Ms. Rikter tells you to do something, you don't talk back. You say, 'how high'? And just do it."

Ellis noticed a slight twitch in the tiger's front paw. *Uh-oh. This could go bad quickly.* He stepped to the front of the fridge lid, and screeched.

Kazi turned his head to the guard, puzzled. "What mean, 'how high?'"

"Kazi," Ms. Rikter said. "I appreciate your skills, your concern, and your willingness to step in and care for Kasool. But please come out. I have notified Dr. Ballmer, and he is on his way there now. He can finish up."

"No need," Kazi said. "Finished now." He grabbed a pair of scissors and snipped the loose ends of the thread.

Kasool growled, and before Kazi could react, rolled over, trapping the man's legs under the massive paws.

"Shit," The guard said, dropping the phone to the floor.

Ellis/Tumbili screeched loudly, and leapt from the fridge lid, easily covering the distance in the air, to the side of the cage, not far from Kasool's head. His fingers and toes latched onto the metal caging, and he rocked himself back and forth, screaming into the tiger's ear as loud as he could—for all his little monkey lungs were worth.

The groggy tiger turned her head and roared at Ellis. The sound in the small cement room was tremendous. Fighting every urge to jump away, Ellis kept screaming back at Kasool. *I wonder what the real Tumbili would do right now.* He worked at being as annoying as possible to get the tiger's attention, considering that to be his only option in this situation, and he was relentless in that quest. His screeches were ear-splitting, and he did not let up.

Ms. Rikter's frantic voice could be heard from the phone on the floor. "Oh my God. What's happening?"

The frightened guard finally pulled his stick, and proceeded to bang it against the corner of the cage. "Heeyah," he screamed. "Heeyah. Get off him."

Kazi, hadn't reacted at all. His legs pinned under the weight of Kasool's front paws, he kept his arms poised behind him, eyes fixed on the sluggish tiger, prepared to make whatever move he needed to survive.

All of the noise seemed to finally have its intended effect. Kasool roared again, even louder, jumped up, and turned her attention back to Ellis/Tumbili. She spoke in her low, growly, feminine voice. "Why are you even still here? You don't belong here. You're not one of us."

Ellis stopped screeching. He clung to the side of the cage and stared deep into Kasool's angry eyes. *I think she is talking to me.*

Kazi slid away quickly, using his arms to drag himself backward toward the door.

When Kasool turned her head toward the man, Ellis attempted to challenge her. He thought if he could understand Kasool's words, perhaps she could understand his. He started to screech once more, but put effort into forming a distinct message. *"Hey, you big striped turd. How dare you talk to me like that. You don't know anything about me or what I've gone through, nor do you know how much I loved her. So you have no right to judge me or…"* Ellis didn't get a chance to finish the thought.

As if it were a lightning strike, Kasool roared again. "I said, *leave us.*" She slashed forward with her huge paw and hit the cage where Ellis/Tumbili was hanging, sending the little monkey flying backward.

He hit the side of the fridge and dropped hard to the cold cement floor.

8

His head hit hard, and the bowl of cereal clattered to the floor, spilling the soggy, milky, mess all over the hardwood floor of the kitchen.

"Oh my word!"

Ellis recognized the voice of Strawberry, odd as that sounded—the startled cry of a woman in her sixties.

"Are you all right?"

He opened his eyes and saw the cat standing over him. Without speaking, he raised himself, and sat up in the milk puddle. He rested his elbows on his knees, and his throbbing head in his hands.

"Mmmmm," Strawberry was lapping at the milk. "You'll need, mmmm, help cleaning, mmmm, this mess up."

Rhubarb sauntered over and joined her. "Into everybody's life a little milk must spill." Then he too went to work, doing his best to clean the milk and the cereal with his tongue.

"What happened to them?" Ellis said, almost too tired to speak.

"Mmmm, what?" Rhubarb said, between licks.

"Kazi and Tumbili. Are they safe? Did they get away from Kasool?"

Strawberry and Rhubarb did not look up, nor did they acknowledge him. They continued lapping unabated at the milk and cereal.

"For Pete's sake!" Ellis slapped his hand down with a loud smack, spattering them both with milk. Strawberry and Rhubarb jerked back. "Are Kazi and Tumbili safe?"

"I don't know who Tumbili is, but yes, Kazi is safe and unhurt." Rhubarb said.

"What do you mean you don't know who Tumbili is? He's the monkey...you know, the monkey you turned me into."

"I didn't think his name was Tumbili," Strawberry said. "But yes, he's safe too. He was just a little shook up."

"Who was Kasool talking to, me or Tumbili?"

Both animals stopped licking the floor and looked up at him. "Kasool spoke?" Rhubarb said.

"Yes. She looked me right in the eye and said that everyone has lost someone and that I shouldn't be hiding away. Said I make her sick. Asked me why I was there. Told me I didn't belong there, and to leave."

Rhubarb and Strawberry looked at each other, as astonished, as cats and dogs could possibly look.

"What?" Ellis asked.

"It's possible that Kasool knew it was you and not…who did you say? Tumbili?" Strawberry said. "We just didn't know the…inter-pet, extended to our exotic friends as well."

Ellis twisted to all fours and clumsily climbed back to his feet. He put his hand on the chair to steady himself until the room leveled out. He unbuttoned his soaked shirt, tossed it in the kitchen sink, grabbed the roll of paper towels, and came back to the table. "Okay, you two. I'm completely confused. I lost my wife. I'm trying to grieve her loss the only way I know how. Though it's not the way you think I should be doing it, so you send me on these journeys to teach me…what? That everybody has shit?" He lowered himself to the floor, tore off several sheets of paper towel, and proceeded to wipe up the mess. "Because, from where I am, stitching up a bleeding tiger doesn't teach me a damn thing." He tossed the soggy towels into the bowl and set it on the table. "But it's already dark outside, so it is making the day go faster. That's a plus for me. If we can keep this up through tomorrow," he said, tearing off four more sheets, "mission accomplished."

Rhubarb sat back on his haunches. "There you are, still concentrating on what you've lost. You refuse to see not only what you *have* in your life, but the fact that there are others hurting who could use your help."

"Well, I don't know anything about taking care of tigers, or monkeys, or goats, or even how to do yoga. So if they need my help they're barking up the wrong tree." Ellis threw the last of the wet paper towels in the bowl and stood, chuckling at his own joke. He set the bowl in the kitchen and walked into the bedroom. Strawberry and Rhubarb followed.

"It doesn't have anything to do with stitching up tigers, or doing yoga," Strawberry said. "What if we were to tell you that Kazi is gay?"

Ellis shrugged his shoulders. "I don't care if he's gay." He unzipped his wet trousers and pulled them off.

"His home country does," Rhubarb said. "Kazi was a very well-respected veterinarian in Kenya. But it is illegal to be gay there. When they were discovered, his partner was arrested and put in prison."

"You've got to be kidding."

"He's not kidding," Strawberry said. "Kazi fled the country, paid his way onto a cargo ship, and was smuggled into the US. He's an illegal immigrant. Friends talked to friends, and he was able to find someone willing to help him here in Iowa. In return, he lives and works at the zoo."

"He *lives* there too?"

"Yes. He has a small cot that he has put in the back room behind the spider monkey cage. That little guy, you called Tumbili, is the best friend he has anymore."

"Huh." Ellis wrapped a robe around him and sat down. "That's too bad."

"Kind of makes you think, doesn't it?" Rhubarb said.

Ellis nodded. "Yes, it does. And you're right, everybody's got shit. But what's also true is that we all have to get through our shit the best way we know how." He stood, walked over and dropped onto the bed. "And my way is to drop out of life for a while."

"Ellis, you can't be serious," Strawberry said.

"I'm very serious." Ellis pulled the covers up. "It's nine o'clock and I'm turning in. You may want to do the same. Santa won't come if you're awake."

Strawberry jumped up on the bed. "Then you have one more trip to take."

Ellis sat up. "No. Stop. I've played your game all day. I'm done. Leave me alone."

"Ellis, I need you to remember something," Rhubarb said. "They're all connected. Remember that. They are all connected. You will have to follow the connections."

"They're all connected? What the hell does that me...." Ellis's head started spinning. His eyesight blurred into a massive swish-pan. Then all went black. He slumped down onto his pillow, and was out once more.

9

His eyes opened to a new dimly-lit world. One tiny light off in the distance illuminated the thin, white, vertical bars filling his vision. Looking around, he saw he was surrounded by the bars.

I'm in a cage. What have they done to me now?

Ellis looked at his hands…not hands. Paws. With five little tiny claws on each of them. Looking down his long, gray furry body, he saw a rather short black tail at the end.

I'm too big to be a hamster or a rat. But I can't be a cat. Why would a cat be in a cage?

Scanning his tiny prison, Ellis noticed there was a small ramp that led to a lower level. He jumped up and scampered down, only to find another level or floor, and another ramp. Beyond that, another floor and another ramp led down to the bottom, a level which had a water bottle attached to the side of the cage and an assortment of balls scattered around the floor. There was a plush football and a small stuffed baseball. There were three plastic balls that had little tinkly bells inside them; one green, one red, and one yellow. And there was a clear rubber ball, with LED circuitry inside. Ellis flicked at it with his paw. It rolled across the cage floor flashing in all sorts of colors. He chuckled, finding this extremely exciting. Clutching the ball awkwardly in his front paws, he crawled up the series of ramps, all the way to the top, then let the ball roll down. It bounced off the bars of the cage, flashing frantically, coming to rest on the second level. Ellis swatted at it, and banked it off the side of the cage, down the last ramp.

Ellis sighed, delighted at the experience, which was incredibly more satisfying than he would have suspected. At that moment he realized exactly what he was.

I'm a ferret!

Though he'd never had a ferret himself, nor did he ever know anybody who did, Ellis remembered heading into a pet shop with Cheri, when they were talking about getting a dog, and seeing a big bin of the frisky little critters, and finding them incredibly cute. They had contemplated getting one but took a hard pass when they talked to the pet store guy who told them ferrets like to chew on pretty much everything, and then hide the objects. Recalling that conversation, the cage made sense to him.

Ellis put his whiskers through the bars to get a glimpse of the person whom his ferret-self shared this life with. The world outside the cage was a rather dark one. The light he could see by was a small fluorescent over a sink. His cage was situated in a corner of a small kitchen. Dirty dishes filled the sink and the counter. A small desk sat next to his cage. On it was a closed laptop, surrounded by piles of mail, mostly unopened.

A counter with a flattop stove faced a dark area. At the end was the faint glow of a large window, looking yellow, probably due to the harsh light of halogen parking lot lights.

A voice said something in the distance—in another room. It grew louder. There was laughter and the jingle of keys. The distinct sound of a key entering a lock, a click, and the door burst open. A woman entered, laughing loudly. "Oh my God. That is so embarrassing."

Ellis watched her through the bars of his cage. She appeared to be of Asian descent, not very tall, with long straight dark hair. She placed an opened box with torn Christmas wrapping on her kitchen counter, unslung her purse and tossed it on the chair next to the desk. "I'm not sure how you do it, girl. You have like, unlimited energy and stamina." She pulled off her winter coat and let it drop in a heap next to the door. She wore a well-tailored green dress, with Christmas tree earrings, and red high-heeled shoes. "And I think that if a kid of mine farted that loud in a restaurant, I would probably just crawl under the table and die." She turned on the lights, walked over, and plugged in a single strand of multi-colored Christmas lights that encircled the window. Though she was dressed like one of Santa's elves, other than that meager display of lights, her apartment was lacking any kind of holiday spirit. She walked over and dropped wearily into a chair. "No. I couldn't do it. I just left the most lame work party, that I couldn't get out of fast enough, and now I'm going to veg the rest of the night away. Probably go to bed early."

Now that the room lights were on, Ellis could see the rest of the space. It appeared to be a small, but upscale apartment. There was a nice recliner sitting across from a large leather couch. A gas fireplace was inset into the wall with a man-sized television hanging above it. However, the walls were white and barren. There were no pictures hung, nor were there any pictures sitting on the tables or the desk.

"Thanks, but I'm going over to my Mom's and spend the day with her. We don't see each other too much now that she's got a new boyfriend, so it will be nice to spend some time together again."

Not only were there dirty dishes on the kitchen counter, there were several plates, and empty wine glasses on the coffee table in front of the couch. Empty wine bottles sat on the floor around the chair.

"Thanks, Sweetie. Same to you. Tell James and the kids Merry Christmas too." She chuckled. "All right. Love you. Bye." The woman clicked off the phone, cradled it with both hands in her lap, and wept. Her shoulders shook slightly and she was quiet, but a slow wail grew. She cried, as if she had just received terrible news, and was now reeling from some remarkable tragedy.

What happened? She was just happy and laughing.

Working hard at catching her breath and gathering herself, the woman lifted the phone, stared at it, then screwed her face into an angry scowl, screamed, and threw it hard at the couch. It bounced off the leather and clattered to the floor. She stood, and with a snarl, kicked it to the corner of the apartment. She picked the Christmas box off the counter, lifted out a bottle of perfume, and with a disgusted scoff, stepped on the pedal of the trash can. The top flipped up and she jammed the perfume and box inside. She had to push down with all her weight behind her, to cram it in far enough for the top to close again. She stood up, wiped her eyes with both hands and looked over at Ellis...the ferret.

He pulled back from the bars and crouched in the corner of the cage. *Uh oh. What am I in for now?*

She smiled at him. "Hi, Hudu." She walked over and opened his cage. Grabbing him by the scruff of his neck, she lifted him out and cradled him in her arms. "You're the brightest spot in my whole life. Do you know that?" Then she scratched his neck and under his chin. It felt remarkable.

Is this how it feels for Strawberry and Rhubarb? Ellis let out a little ferret sigh. *It sure beats being kicked across the room like the phone, which is where I thought this was going.*

She set him down next to an empty bowl on the floor, grabbed the bowl and filled it from a bag that had a picture of a ferret on it, then set it back down in front of him. "Enjoy your dinner, Hudu." She turned and headed out of the kitchen down the hall.

I guess I am hungry. I wonder if this will taste as good as the goat food. After a couple nibbles, he realized it didn't. Deciding he wasn't so hungry after all, he turned to do a little exploring—see why he was there in the first place.

The woman came around the corner, wearing gray sweatpants and a black, Iowa Hawkeyes sweatshirt. She opened a cupboard only to find it empty. Slamming it shut, she grabbed a dirty wine glass from the counter, rinsed it out, and wiped it clean with a paper towel, which she dropped on the counter. Pulling a bottle of wine out of another cupboard, the woman sat at the little desk, opened her laptop, and filled the wine glass. After taking a long drink she started typing furiously, stopping here and there to take more long drinks from her glass. The glass would empty, and she would fill it, and drain it again.

Ellis/Hudu rounded the kitchen counter and found a long tube lying along the wall. Unable to resist, he headed in and raced down to the round circle of light at the end. He came out in front of the doorway to what looked sort of like a bedroom. There was a big bed sitting in it, surrounded by huge piles of clothes, all at least twice his ferret-height in size. On top of the closest pile was the green dress she was just wearing. She was the messiest person Ellis had ever seen in his entire life.

Cheri wouldn't be able to take two steps into this apartment without having to pick things up and start dusting.

Running back out into the living room, he saw a large green stuffed turtle with an open mouth. Again, unable to resist, he rushed across the room, hopping over pizza boxes and around Chinese take-out containers to jump inside. It was soft, and warm, and it felt like a place his ferret-self liked to spend time.

From this new vantage point he scanned the room. There were more wine bottles, cans of beer, and empty prescription pill bottles lying on the floor.

I think this girl has serious problems.

Just then the woman stood up from her desk and wiped her eyes once more. Taking a deep breath, she collected herself and walked back down the hall.

Ellis wanted to get a closer look at what she'd been working on. He crept out of the turtle's mouth, scurried across the floor and looked down the hall. He could see her standing in the room at the end of the hall, which he could tell was the bathroom. She had several pill bottles sitting on the counter and was closely studying the label of another.

Ellis continued on. He jumped up on the chair, then up onto the desktop. Careful not to touch a single key on the keyboard, he sat next to her laptop and craned his neck over, so he could read it clearly.

I am writing this on Christmas Eve. It is a night when the whole world is singing, smiling, happy, dreaming, in love.

But I am not. Once again I find myself completely and utterly despondent.

Five minutes ago I hung up the phone with my best friend. I laughed, told her Merry Christmas, and that I loved her. But the truth is that I wanted to scream at her. Tell her I hated her. I can't stand her. I revile the fact that she is happy, she is in love, and she has beautiful kids, and it all makes me sick.

In all honesty she is a wonderful person—very giving, supportive, delightful, and she deserves all the happiness in this world.

But I can't get there. I am forever held down. Like I'm chained to a huge rock of despair. I cannot break the chains. I have tried. I have actually been able to stretch them from time to time. Found myself in wonderful relationships, and balanced briefly on the edge of true happiness. But the chains always coil back in, dragging me back into the darkness. And the relationships wither and die, like beautiful flowers kept in a closet.

For years it has been hard. Just to get out of bed. To get to work and be productive at all. Let alone have any kind of real conversation with anyone.

I have always told myself to survive. Just make it through the next day. But once that day is done, all I have to look forward to is another day just like it. There is no payoff for making it through each day. Not when the next day promises the exact same kind of pain. And the day after that. And the day after that. And the day after that.

So when I started contemplating the thought of stopping my next days altogether, I started to feel real peace. A calm down deep in my soul. I have done my best to keep up appearances for everyone else through the holiday season, but now it's Christmas Eve, the parties are over, and nobody is concerned with me anymore.

Now is my time. And I plan to make use of it.

When you think of me, please don't feel sad. On the contrary, my heart will finally be calm and at peace. My only wish is that someone accept Hudu into their life, and care and love him as much as I have. He is my one true joy. I promise he will be yours too.

To all of my family and friends, thank you for being in my life. I wish you all the best.

Peace.

Kimber

"Hudu, what are you doing?"

Ellis/Hudu spun around, startled that he'd been caught. The woman named Kimber was standing by the kitchen counter, where she had just placed a bottle of pills.

She plans on killing herself tonight, and she's going to use the pills in that bottle to do it.

"Why did you just look like you were reading that? You silly little guy." She picked him up, stepped back, leaned against the counter, and snuggled him close. "Did you read where I said you were my one true joy in this life? I meant it."

Now I know why I'm here. I need to stop her.

Kimber scratched him under the chin and kissed the top of his head.

Distracted by the sheer delightfulness of the touch, it took Ellis a moment to remember his mission. She was standing right next to the counter where she had set the pills. He wouldn't have a better chance than that very moment.

Ellis dug his little claws into her sweatshirt and climbed up onto her shoulder. He looked down and caught a glimpse of the pill bottle.

"Hey, buddy. Where are you going?" She grasped him around his belly and dragged him back down.

Ellis's chance was slipping away. He needed to do something fast.

I'm sorry about this, Miss Kimber.

Bending his remarkably flexible spine, he coiled around and sunk his teeth into the index finger of her right hand. She cried out and released her grip. Ellis clambered up onto her shoulder and dropped to the counter.

Kimber shook her hand, turned around, and stepped back. "Shit, Hudu. Not you too."

Ellis/Hudu did not hesitate. He clamped his teeth onto the edge of the pill bottle and scampered across the landscape of dirty dishes.

"Hey, wait. Hudu, no!"

Coming to the far edge of the counter, Ellis did not even slow down. *I hope these guys can land like cats.* Not even close. He dropped like a stone, hit the floor hard, and lost his grip on the pill bottle. It bounced several feet away.

"Bad, Hudu. No."

From the corner of his eye, he could see Kimber heading toward him. But even though he knocked out what little air there was in a ferret body, he didn't have the option to slow down.

Kimber reached for the pill bottle, but Ellis/Hudu covered the distance in one jump. He latched his teeth around the top once again and shot under the big leather sofa.

"Hudu, *stop!*"

Kimber was now clearly angry, but he didn't care. This was what he was here for, and he was going to make sure this girl survived Christmas. He ran to the center of the couch and stopped to catch his breath. He looked back and saw knees hit the floor. Kimber's head dropped into view, and she looked right at him, scowling. "Hudu, you bring those back to me right this very minute."

When he didn't budge she growled and stood. Her feet walked out of view and he heard a door open. Ellis crawled to the edge of the sofa and peered out. He saw Kimber pull her hand out of a closet in the hallway, brandishing a broom.

Oh crap. I guess I didn't think this through well enough.

He ran back to the bottle and clamped his teeth around the edge of the cap once again. He readied himself, watching her feet come around.

Kimber's knees touched down at the direct center, in front of the couch. An excellent choice. She could cover the whole area from there. Ellis turned and ran back the way he'd come. Before he reached freedom, the broom handle collided hard with his side. He cried out, and rolled with it, but the bottle of pills was knocked out of his mouth and swept out from under the couch.

Kimber's hands and feet crawled toward the bottle.

Wincing from the pain in his back, Ellis/Hudu ran as fast as he could. Before Kimber's hand had a chance to clasp around the pill bottle, he shot out from under the couch and snatched it in his mouth once again.

"Dammit, Hudu. Stop!" She sounded desperate.

He didn't slow. He needed to find a place to take this thing that she couldn't reach with a broom.

Coming around the far end of the couch, he saw the small opening of the tube that he'd crawled through earlier. With Kimber right behind him, he charged for the opening.

Just as he entered, he was yanked to a stop. Kimber had managed to grab his tail and pull him back out of the tube. Digging his little claws into the grooves in the edge of the slinky-like tubing, he held out for a mere moment, but he did not have the strength of a full-sized human. He lost his grip and was dragged backward. Releasing the bottle, he did the only thing left to him at that point. He reached around and bit her hand once again, this time sinking his teeth in deep. She screamed, released her grip, then let loose with a tirade of profanity.

With the sides of the tube a frosted plastic, Ellis watched her dark form stomp into the bathroom. Listened while she sobbed and opened a drawer. He heard the sound of a band-aid package ripped open. After a moment she stomped past him once more, headed to the front door area for a minute, then came back.

"Okay, you little shit. Time to give it up."

Uh-oh. This doesn't sound good.

Kimber grabbed the flexible tube in the middle and lifted it up, shaking it hard. Ellis clutched at the grooves, but he couldn't hold on and still keep the pill bottle in his mouth. It bounced out of the tube and onto the floor.

Kimber reached down and snatched it up. "Got it."

Ellis heard it set back down on the counter. Then the tubing was dragged into the kitchen. One end was placed inside the door of the cage, and Kimber shook furiously.

Try as he might to stay inside, Ellis/Hudu finally lost his grip, tumbled out of the tube and into the cage once more. Before he had a chance to regain his feet, the door to the cage was slammed shut.

Ellis spun around, stuck his nose through the thin white bars and looked up into the sad eyes of Kimber.

Tears streamed down her face. She dropped to her knees in front of him, her hands now had big fluffy mittens on them. "If I didn't know better, I'd think you were trying to keep me from doing what I really need to do." She cried harder. "It makes me feel good to think that anyway…to think there is actually somebody around who cares if I'm here or not. So even though you bit me twice, I want to thank you for being a friend to me and putting a smile on my face so many times, when I thought my face didn't even make that shape anymore." Kimber stood. "But I need to do this now, and I can't with you looking at me like that." She grabbed the cage with her mittened hands and rolled it across the kitchen floor.

Crap. This is on wheels. Why didn't I notice that before?

Ellis pleaded with her. "Don't do this, Kimber. You can call me. I can put you in touch with my grief counselor. You have options." But all it came out as strange ferret chattering, which for some reason, made Kimber cry even harder.

She rolled the cage into the closet in the hall.

Ellis/Hudu scurried to the top level of the cage and clung to the bars. "Don't do this, Kimber," he cried out in the strange noises of a ferret.

Kimber stepped back. "Goodbye, best friend." She wiped her tear-filled eyes and shut the door, leaving him in total darkness.

10

"Kimber, no. Don't do this!" Ellis shot upright in bed. He scanned the room, surprised to see light again. It took him another moment to realize he was back in his bedroom. His heart thumped in his chest, and his shirt was wet with sweat. He ran his fingers through his damp hair and looked around for his pets. "Strawberry. Rhubarb. I'm back." Neither animal came in to see him.

Ellis threw the covers off and hopped out of bed. "We need to talk. This is an emergency." In the kitchen he saw Rhubarb lying in his basket. "Rhubarb." Ellis knelt by the old dog. "You have to tell me where to find her…that…that girl, named Kimber. I think she's going to kill herself. Tonight."

Rhubarb lifted his head lazily, opened his mouth and started panting.

Ellis dropped to both knees. "What are you waiting for, boy? Tell me how to find her. I have to go over there, *right now.*"

Rhubarb reached his head back and nibbled at an itch on his leg.

"Oh, come on," Ellis said. Something nudged him. He looked down and saw Strawberry performing her usual stop-what-you're-doing-and-give-me-some-love routine. "Strawberry, thank God." He picked her up and spoke directly into her face. "The owner of the ferret you just sent me to, is getting ready to kill herself. I need you to tell me where she is. I need to go stop her. Maybe I can talk to her, or something."

The only response from Strawberry was a soft purring sound.

"You've got to be kidding me. Now you stop talking? You couldn't have stopped with the stupid goat?"

Rhubarb slowly climbed out of his basket and walked over to the back door.

"A woman is getting ready to kill herself right this very minute, and all you want to do is pee?"

Rhubarb let out a small whine and shuffled his feet.

Ellis looked back and forth to the cat and the dog. "Are you telling me you're not talking now? Either of you?" He set Strawberry back down on the floor. The cat immediately rubbed against his leg and purred. "What the hell happened?"

Another high-pitched whine. Ellis rushed over and slid the door open. Rhubarb stepped out a few feet and lifted his leg against a planter.

Ellis sighed. "Great. Just go right there, Rhubarb." He closed the door and rushed back into the bedroom, talking to himself all the way. "They couldn't have picked a worse time to ditch me. What do I do?" He grabbed a fresh pair of jeans from the closet and pulled them up. "Wait. What did Rhubarb say? They're all connected." Ellis grabbed a blue and gray flannel shirt off the treadmill and walked into the bathroom. He looked in the mirror and put the shirt on. "What was it he said? 'They're all connected.' But he said something else too." Grabbing a comb, he did his best to straighten the mostly gray mess on the top of his head. "I have to follow the connections." Ellis threw the comb down on the counter. "He said I have to follow the connections. But what does that mean? Do I have to start at the ranch and work my way through them all? She could be dead by then." Ellis turned, headed back into the kitchen, and let Rhubarb back in. "I wish you could just answer one question for me, boy. If they're all connected which one do I start with?" Ellis closed the door. "Wait! If they're all connected, then it doesn't matter which one I start with. I start with the closest one." He grabbed his wallet and keys off the counter, grabbed his coat off the hook, and ran out the door.

11

Stepping out of his house was like stepping through a portal into Christmastown. A light snow drifted down in the crisp night air. The houses all along the street were lit with strings of bright, twinkly, Christmas lights, making Ellis's unlit house look like a missing tooth. The neighbors had music playing through outdoor speakers, currently featuring Trans-Siberian Orchestra's, "Christmas Canon." It was the kind of night that existed only in the cheesy holiday movies that yoga-Julia was watching, and to be fair, Cheri used to watch as well. And it was precisely the kind of night that Ellis wanted to avoid. His first reaction to stepping into the magic of such a night, was to turn around and grab Cheri. If she were here, they would be walking, gloved hand in gloved hand, down the road, and experiencing the beauty and the quiet of a brisk December eve. The only sounds would be the music and Cheri's sweet voice as she pointed out the decorations that she thought were the most beautiful.

Then the peace and serenity were destroyed by a distant shout. "Porter, you asshole!" Ellis looked across the street to see Perry Mueller leaning out his open front door. "I catch you ever talking like that to my wife again and making her cry, I'll come over there and kick your ass. Christmas or no Christmas. You got that?"

Ellis climbed into his blue Chevy Equinox as fast as he could and slammed the door, shutting out the wonder and the angst. "Good God. Has he been waiting at his front door all night for me to walk outside?" Ellis turned the key and sped away.

It took much less time than usual to drive to Billing Park Zoo. A combination of very sparse traffic on Christmas Eve, and his own heavy foot got him there in just over five minutes.

The holiday ambiance was even worse at the zoo. Billing Park had their legendary Christmas light show beaming. It was his neighborhood on steroids—it had to be easily visible on satellite photos. They added the family touches, such as blow-up reindeer, and elves everywhere, and a large Santa at the front gate greeting visitors as they came in. It was an attempt to make the zoo the place to be for families, even in the bitter cold of winter.

Ellis didn't park in the lot. He drove up to the entrance, hopped out, and ran to the closed bars of the gate screaming. "Kazi. Kazi, I need you." He walked back and forth, in front of the gate, and waved to the camera, hoping somebody would hear, or see him. "Kazi. Can you hear me?"

After a few minutes, Ellis heard an angry man's voice. "What the hell?" He looked to see the security guard, with the red hair and the untucked shirt walking up the lane, breath fogging out in front of him.

Ellis grabbed the bars and stuck his face through, feeling very much like Hudu, the ferret. "I need to speak with Kazi. It's very urgent. Can you get him for me?"

At 20 feet away the guard stopped, and his eyes blinked several times. "Ahh, I'm the only one here. I don't know a Kazi."

Ellis remembered Strawberry had talked about Kazi being an undocumented immigrant. That was why the guard was thrown off. He stepped back and spoke calmly. "Look, I know he's here. I know he worked on a tiger tonight, and you were with him. I need to speak with him about another matter entirely. Please let me see him."

"Holy shit," the guard said. He pulled a phone out of his pocket, hit the screen and held it up to his ear. "Ahhh, I'm sorry to bother you again, Ms. Rikter, but there is a guy standing at the gate here right now, and he wants to see Kazi." The guard nodded and swung around. Though he now spoke quieter, Ellis could still make out a portion of the conversation. "…know, but he...Kasool and...urgent." The guard waited a moment, then spun back around. "Who are you with?"

"I'm not *with* anybody," Ellis said. "But I desperately need his help."

"He says he's not with anybody. He just needs to talk to Kazi." After a moment the guard nodded. "Okay, here ya go." He walked to the gate and handed the phone through the bars. "This is Ms. Rikter. She runs the zoo, and she wants to talk to you."

Ellis grabbed the phone. "Hello."

"Hello. Who is this?" the woman's voice on the other end said.

"I'm Ellis Porter."

"Hello, Mr. Porter. I'm Laura Rikter, and I'm the Director of the Billing Park Zoo. I understand you want to speak with Kazi. Can I ask you what this is regarding, and how you know him?"

And there was the question. Perhaps it had cropped up in the back of Ellis's mind, but in all of his haste to get going so he could try to do something to stop Kimber, he had never really given it much thought. What was he supposed to say? Should he tell this woman that he'd been in the head of the monkey, and met Kazi that way? That his cat and his dog had been talking to him all day and introduced them? How would she respond to any of that? Would she thank him for letting her know, and then have the geeky guard introduce them? Ellis was pretty sure it wouldn't play out that way.

"Hello?" Laura Rikter said.

"I just know," he finally said.

"Okay. I need you to be straight with me right now." He could hear the anxiety in her voice. "Are you with ICE? If you are, I want to be very clear, this was *my* decision, and *my* decision only. Do not penalize the zoo, or any of the employees for my choices. I am the director, and I forced the issue here. They didn't have a say."

Ellis respected her sense of accountability and her loyalty to her employees. He wanted to ease her fears, especially if it would get him to Kazi sooner. "No, Ms. Rikter. I am not with ICE, or any law enforcement agency. I have a quick question for Kazi, and then I will be on my way. And no, I won't tell anybody else that Kazi is here either. As far as I know there isn't anybody else who knows about him, and nobody will hear it from me."

After a short pause, Laura Rikter said, "Very well. Put Jenkins back on."

"Thank you…uh…Merry Christmas."

"Merry Christmas to you, Mr. Porter."

Ellis handed the phone to the guard, who now had a name. He put the phone to his ear and listened as she gave him his marching orders. "Sure thing, Ms. Rikter.

Sorry to bother you again. Merry Christmas." Jenkins put the phone in his coat pocket, sniffled, and pulled on a set of keys tethered to his belt. He unlocked the large gate and swung it open, jerking his head for Ellis to enter.

"Thank you," Ellis said, scooting through. He waited for Jenkins to lock the gate once more and then lead him into the zoo.

Ellis hadn't been to Billing Park in years; not since the girls were very young. He remembered special activities like the summer campouts on the zoo grounds. He couldn't help but smile recalling the early morning in their tent. Cassie and Katie were sleeping soundly in their sleeping bags until the lion woke up and let the world know it was time to rise, with a blood curdling roar. Both Cassie and Katie screamed and crawled into bed with Cheri and him.

Passing by the elaborately decorated cages, he also recalled the many visits they made to the zoo during the holiday season, visiting Santa and drinking cocoa, all while seeing a few animals too. He didn't think the girls ever made it home without having to throw their winter coats in the wash to get off all the spilled cocoa.

Jenkins stopped at the back door of the primate house, unlocked it, walked in, and held the door open for Ellis.

Ellis nodded his thanks and Jenkins grunted a "Yeah" back. Leading him down a narrow cement block hall, much like the one Ellis had seen while in Tumbili's head, he stopped at a door, opened it a crack and stuck his head in. "Hey, Kazi, you decent? You got a visitor." Jenkins opened the door further and gestured for Ellis to enter.

Inside on a cot, next to a cage which housed a small spider monkey, lay the African man named Kazi. He was snuggled in a sleeping bag, leaning on one elbow, with an ice pack across his ribs. Apparently Kasool had done a little damage after all.

Ellis stared at the man a moment. He was much more diminutive than he had appeared when Ellis, as a small spider monkey, sat on his shoulder. He lay there in a white t-shirt. A large blue duffel bag sat under his cot, flaps of clothes spewing out in all directions. It probably consisted of everything he owned. The overalls he had been wearing were folded loosely at his feet. This man's whole life was now this zoo—his only companion, the spider monkey in the cage next to him, who apparently escorted him whenever he left this room. All because being gay in his own country was considered a criminal act.

The man named Kazi sat up slowly, his eyes wide with trepidation, most assuredly fearful of his precarious position as an illegal immigrant.

Ellis stepped in and held out his hand. "Hello, Kazi. My name is Ellis Porter. It's a pleasure to meet you."

Kazi looked at his hand, and then up at Jenkins.

"He's only here to talk about something. That's all," Jenkins said.

Kazi shook his hand. "Hello, Mr. Porter." He braced himself on the cot and pushed himself up, wincing as he did so.

Ellis put a hand on his shoulder. "Please, don't get up. I see you're in a little bit of pain, and I only need a moment of your time."

Kazi lowered himself again and Ellis sat next to him. "This may seem like a strange question, but do you happen to know a woman, named Kimber, who owns a ferret named Hudu?"

Kazi looked back up at Jenkins, his face a mixture of fear and confusion.

"Are you kidding me?" Jenkins said. "You were screaming and hollering at the front gate for a stupid question like that?"

"I know it sounds odd," Ellis said. "But her life may depend on me getting to her apartment as soon as possible."

Kazi shook his head. "I do not know any woman with a ferret."

"Okay, you asked your question," Jenkins held the door open. "He doesn't know her, so let's let him rest. He's had a big night."

"Wait." Ellis held up a hand. "It's very important that I find her. How about a rancher? Do you know any ranchers?"

Kazi shook his head again.

"C'mon," Jenkins said.

"How about a goat-yoga instructor, with a goat named Deepak?"

Kazi looked up at Jenkins and then back to Ellis. He slowly nodded. "I know a woman named Julia, with a goat named Deepak. She lives in a barn."

"Holy shit," Jenkins said, and he let the door close with a heavy clunk.

Ellis could hardly believe his ears. Rhubarb told him they were all connected. And now the first connection had materialized. "How do you know her?"

"The woman who run this zoo. She is a friend. She takes classes there. Deepak was sick. She had me go over and see the goat. Make him well."

"Then I have to go see her next." Ellis stood. "Do you recall the name of the yoga barn?"

Kazi reached over and grabbed his overalls. "Shanti. It is called Shanti, Yoga Barn." He threw his sleeping bag cover off him and put his legs in his trousers.

"It's all right, Kazi. I'll try to find the place myself." Ellis gestured for him to stay. "I have GPS on my phone. You can rest."

Kazi looked up at him. "You're going to see Julia?"

Ellis nodded. "Yes, I am."

"This is matter of life and death, for the woman with the ferret?"

Ellis nodded again. "I have every indication to believe that. Yes."

Kazi pulled his pant legs up. "Then I will go with you. You are a strange man, and you may frighten Miss Julia."

Jenkins snickered. "You got that right."

"She will not be frightened of me. And perhaps I can be of help to the woman with the ferret."

Ellis sighed. He had to admit, Kazi was probably right on both accounts. "Okay. I appreciate any help you can give me."

12

The GPS said the Shanti Yoga Barn was a seventeen-minute drive from the zoo. Ellis knew the area. It was just outside of town, not too far from the expressway.

The drive was quiet. Kazi's gaze was fixed out his side of the window at the fast food signs, and Christmas decorations that flew by. Ellis thought how everything must appear so foreign to him, coming from an African country. But then realized he really knew nothing about Africa and considered the fact that McDonald's and Taco Bell had probably invaded his continent by now too. "How long have you been here?" He asked.

Kazi looked over. "I have been in your country about four months. I have been in my room at the zoo about two and a half months."

Ellis nodded. He wanted to know more about this man's story but didn't know how to ask, knowing that he already knew more than he should about a complete stranger. And, quite frankly, it was probably more than Kazi wanted to share. "So...what brought you to Iowa?"

"I rode in a truck from New Jersey."

"No, no." Ellis shook his head. "I mean why did you pick Iowa to come to stay?"

"Oh, yes." Kazi nodded. "I had a friend of the family that works in your Customs office. She helped me. She knew Ms. Rikter. Knew I could handle zoo animals. Ms. Rikter has been very nice to me. And I like the zoo very much."

"So is that where you live?" Ellis asked. "In that room with the monkey?"

"Yes. It is very comfortable." Kazi said. He looked back out the window. "And I like the monkey very much."

"It's good to have friends." Ellis nodded. The conversation lapsed. But Ellis didn't like the quiet. Now that he had another individual within conversation distance, he didn't want there to be awkward silence. "So, what's the monkey's name?" "Ricky." Kazi still looked out the window.

Ellis didn't understand. He thought that was the same monkey he had been earlier in the evening. But Kazi called him something different. Perhaps that was why Strawberry and Rhubarb were confused. "Ricky, huh? Nice name, I guess."

Kazi scowled and shook his head.

"Oh, you don't like that name?"

"No." Kazi said. "Not at all."

"Do you call it something different?"

Kazi looked back over. "I call him 'Tumbili.'"

"Tumbili," Ellis said. "That's a nice name too. I'm assuming it means something in your language."

"It does." Kazi looked back out the window. "It means, 'monkey.'"

Ellis shrugged. "Makes sense." The remaining twelve minutes passed in silence.

The GPS told them what driveway to pull into. The Shanti Yoga Barn was an actual barn. Though it was night, the structure was lit with a combination of bright outdoor safety lighting, and twinkly white Christmas lights around each of the doors. It had obviously been refurbished, and the entire exterior of the building was painted a bright pastel green, with the word "Shanti" painted in a dark forest green along the side facing the road.

"I wonder what her favorite color is?" Ellis chuckled.

"One would think…green." Kazi said.

Ellis made a mental note that Kazi didn't get sarcasm. He parked in the gravel lot next to the barn and shut off the engine. "I'll go see if there's a doorbell or something. You wait here."

Kazi opened the door, stepped out and closed it.

"Or feel free to come along," Ellis said, opening his door.

As soon as he stepped out, a spotlight clicked on and shone down on both of them. A woman's voice screeched over a loudspeaker. "Stay right there, dirt bags! You know we're not open, so if you take one more step, the police will be here faster than you can say, 'Oh, shit.' This is Christmas Eve. You should be ashamed of yourselves."

Kazi waved his arms to the light. "Miss Julia. It is me, Kazi. I fixed your goat."

"Wait…who's that? Kazi? What the hell…" There was a loud clunking, and a distant, "Oh, shit." Over the loudspeaker. Then the light and the speaker cut out at the same time.

Ellis and Kazi looked at each other and back up at the barn, but they did not dare to take a step. Lights lit windows on the second floor. A few moments later, a light to the side clicked on, and a door opened up. Ellis recognized Julia when she stuck her head out. "Kazi. What are you doing here?"

Kazi pointed at his feet. "May I move now?"

"Yes, yes." Julia waved them over. "Come on in." She held the door for them to enter.

Ellis let Kazi go ahead of him, grateful now for the African's assistance. Julia, still wearing her baggy sweats and fluffy pink socks, greeted Kazi warmly and gave him a hug, then held out her hand to Ellis. "Hi. Julia Madison."

Ellis shook it. "Ellis Porter. Thanks for talking with us."

"No problem. Sorry about all the yelling and the light…"

Ellis waved it off. "Not at all. It's the smart thing to do. You never know who it's going to be."

She turned to Kazi. "What are you doing cruising around on Christmas Eve?"

Kazi gestured toward Ellis. "Mr. Porter is trying to stop a woman from killing herself."

"Oh my word," Julia said. "How can I help?"

Impressed by her concern, Ellis asked, "Do you happen to know a woman named Kimber, who owns a ferret?"

Julia thought a moment. "I have a lot of women who come here, obviously. I'm sure I don't know if any of them own a ferret. At least not that they have mentioned to me anyway."

"How about the name Kimber? She's Asian. Does that name sound familiar?"

Again Julia thought, eyes drifting up as she did. She shook her head. "Nope. I have four Asian women as regular customers and none of them are named Kimber."

Ellis sighed. "Shit."

"What about the rancher?" Kazi said.

"Rancher?" Julia asked.

"Yes. Do you happen to know a rancher named Kobbs?" Ellis asked.

"Yes, Randal Kobbs. He's right up the road." Julia said, pointing her thumb over her shoulder. "He sold me my goat."

Another connection accounted for. "How far up the road?"

"Well, it's a country road so…fifteen, twenty minutes up the road."

Ellis sighed. "Then we'd better get going. Thank you for your help."

"Wait," Julia said. "How do you know this Asian woman is going to kill herself?"

There was the question again. Ellis shrugged. "I guess you could call it a vision."

Julia gasped. "Say no more. Visions can be very powerful things. Please, just give me a sec, and I'll be ready."

"Ready for what?"

Julia smiled at him. "We have a life to save, don't we?" She spun around and jumped the stairs, two at a time.

Ellis looked at Kazi who called after her. "We will wait in the car."

"Okay!" She yelled back down the stairs.

Before they had even reached the car, Julia bolted out of the door and locked it behind her. She now wore yoga pants, boots, a short stylish winter coat, and a stocking cap. She ran over, pulling on big wool mittens.

They all got into the car at the same time. "Turn left out of here, and watch for deer." Julia said.

13

"Isn't this night beautiful? I've just been sitting and looking out the window for, like an hour, at the pretty snowflakes coming down." Once she was around others, Ellis noticed that Julia Madison was incredibly talkative. "So Kazi, after you took care of Deepak, he's been doing great. You know, he *had* lost his appetite, which is why Laura brought you over in the first place. You gave him that smelly mixture, and ever since then he's been eating everything in sight. He chewed through two of my yoga mats in one week."

She talked for the entire twenty minutes it took to drive to the ranch. Ellis wondered how she could possibly be quiet during a meditation session.

Once she was done talking about the weather, and about Deepak, she turned her attention to Ellis. "So this must have been one heck of a vision for you to be dragging people out in the middle of the night on

Christmas Eve. Why is it you think this Kimber is going to kill herself?"

Ellis glanced up at her in the rear-view mirror and wondered how he would answer this. "Well…the whole thing seemed so real."

"Uh-huh. What part?" Julia asked.

"Well…the suicide note."

"Are you telling me you got a vision of the actual note?" Julia shook her shoulders. "Wow. I just got chills."

"Yes. In fact I read it." This was easier than he had anticipated.

"You could see the words? What did it say?"

Kazi looked over at him, curious.

Ellis glanced at both of them. "She talked about…just trying to make it through the next day. And then the next day would be just as hard. And how the thought of stopping all of the days gave her peace."

"Oh, that poor thing."

"Yeah, I know," Ellis said. "She said that those who know her shouldn't feel bad for her. That now she'd not be hurting anymore."

"Okay," Julia said. "We're gonna help this girl." Her finger pointed forward. "Turn right at the next driveway. That's Kobbs's place."

Ellis turned in, and his headlights flashed across the iron arch at the driveway that had the words "Kobbs Ranch" within the ornate decorations. This was definitely the place.

As one would expect with a ranch, the driveway was long and wound around a few bends. His car handled it fairly well in the fresh snow, but Ellis could understand why ranchers usually drove the big four-wheel-drive trucks.

The house was large, elegant, and much like Ellis's house, completely devoid of Christmas decorations of any kind. He pulled into the half circle drive and parked in front of a set of stone steps that led up to a pillared front porch. When the three of them stepped out of the car, the front door opened, and a very imposing figure stepped out, wearing a stained white tank t-shirt, suspenders connected to blue jeans, and bare feet which must have been freezing on the cold cement porch with the thin layer of new snow. The man's hair was matted and messed, and he held a double-barreled shotgun, which he had leveled in their direction. He stepped to the edge of the porch and wobbled a bit. "Unless you're here to sing carols, you'd best get the hell off my land."

They all stopped and raised their hands, standing frozen to the spot for a tense moment, each person contemplating what to do next.

Julia was the first to speak. She waved her arms. "Whoa, Mr. Kobbs. It's me, Julia Madison. I'm the yoga lady who bought your goat."

Kobbs squinted at her, finally showing something akin to recognition. "What is it you want?"

"We're hoping you can help us with something."

Ellis looked up at the old man. He had obviously been drowning his sorrows in some sort of bottle and didn't look like he was in any shape to help at all.

Julia glanced over her shoulder at him. "Ahhh, you're on."

"Oh, okay." Ellis stepped around the front of the car. "Mr. Kobbs. I was wondering if you knew an Asian girl with a ferret."

Kobbs scoffed. "Is this some kind of damn joke?"

"No, sir. We're worried about her and we're trying to find her."

"Do you know her?" Kobbs asked.

Ellis shook his head. "No, I don't. Which is why I thought you'd be able to help."

"You're worried about someone you don't even know?"

"Yes, sir."

There was a pause in the conversation for a moment. A pause in which Kobbs wobbled a little more.

Julia stepped forward. "He had a vision, Mr. Kobbs. He saw this woman's suicide note, and he's afraid she's going to kill herself."

"Oh, for Pete's sake. You're whack jobs."

Ellis couldn't blame the man for thinking this. He knew that if someone came to his door in the middle of the night on Christmas Eve, with a story like this, he'd think the exact same thing.

Kobbs lowered his gun and rubbed his face with his hand. "Well I don't know what vision brought you to me, but I don't know any Asian girl with a ferret. So pack up your crystal balls, and your tarot cards and get the hell off my land."

Kazi, who still had his hands raised, spoke softly. "Her name is Kimber."

"What was that?" Kobbs said. He raised his shotgun once more. "Did you say something?"

Just like with Kasool the African was calm and collected. "Her name is Kimber," he said with an easy tone.

Kobbs placed a bare foot on the top step of the porch. "I don't care what her name is. I don't know an Asian woman with a ferret. Or anybody else with a ferret." He gestured toward the road with his shotgun. "Now get the hell out of here."

Kazi and Julia turned and jumped back in the car slamming their doors.

Ellis hadn't moved. He knew there was nowhere else to go but here. Kimber didn't have a chance if he were to drive away. He had to trust that Strawberry and Rhubarb were right. "Mr. Kobbs, I know this is asking a lot, especially at this late hour. But this girl is in trouble. Could you please just take a moment and…"

"I said," Kobbs cut him off. The old man raised his shotgun, pointed it at Ellis and looked down the barrel. "Get the hell out of here."

Staring down both barrels of a shotgun, pointed directly at him, held by an angry, inebriated old man, was the breaking point for Ellis. At that moment he realized he should be home in bed, taking his medications so he could sleep through Christmas like he had originally planned. He was supposed to wake up on the 26th and find his way back to his life again. Everybody had problems. These three people he was with were definite proof of that. But he wasn't supposed to be the answer to their problems. He had to think about himself. Getting killed over someone he didn't even know, sounded as ridiculous as the story of how he was standing in this old man's driveway to begin with.

Ellis bowed his head. "I'm leaving." He slowly backed up so as not to startle Kobbs. "And I'm very sorry to have bothered you." He rounded the front of his car, Kobbs's shotgun following his every move. When he reached the door, he grabbed the handle. "Merry Christmas, Mr. Kobbs."

The shotgun finally lowered.

He opened the car door, but before he could climb in, Kobbs mumbled. "Kimber Lee Lee."

Ellis stopped and gazed back up at him. The old man had a dazed look on his face. "What was that?"

Kobbs let the gun fall to his side. "There was a young Asian girl who went to our church. Her name was Kimberly Lee, but everyone called her Kimber Lee Lee. One Sunday, a year or so back, she was showing around pictures of some critter she'd just gotten for a pet. I only know that because she showed my wife. Tina came to me and said that Kimber Lee had gotten a rat as a pet." Kobbs's gaze drifted off to the field. "I guess she'd never seen a ferret before. Can't say as I have either." He looked back at Ellis. "I'm sure I have her address in an old church directory. Why don't you come in while I look for it? It's cold as shit out here."

14

The faces in the rear-view mirror couldn't have been more different. Though she was now quiet, Julia still couldn't stop smiling. Ellis thought that if he hadn't been a goat and actually seen her cry, he would think that was her normal face at rest. The woman was truly light-hearted by nature.

But next to her was the hard, craggy face of Kobbs. Though he wasn't scowling, his resting face looked a great deal harsher than the young woman he was sitting next to. Ellis was sure that the man's alcohol intake this evening had something to do with how he looked, and how he felt. It was pretty apparent that sitting in the back seat of a moving vehicle feeling like he did was probably not the best decision he'd made today. But when he discovered Kimberly Lee's address in an old church directory his wife had kept in her office, he felt so bad about how he'd treated them, he said he wanted to come help as well. "Movin' around doin' somethin' is a hell of alot better, than just sittin' around wishin' things were different."

It was a sentiment that Ellis didn't currently ascribe to. And yet, here he was, driving four strangers around at 11:30 on Christmas Eve, going to help another complete stranger. And all because his cat and his dog convinced him to. It was crazy. Ellis shook his head at the ridiculousness of it all.

"Everything okay, Ellis?" Julia asked.

Ellis locked eyes with her in the rear-view mirror. "Yes. Why?"

"I saw you shake your head. I was just wondering if you were getting tired."

"Oh, no, I was…ahhh…yes. I guess I was feeling a little tired." He wondered if he'd ever be able to tell how he really learned about them all.

"Did you need someone else to drive?" Julia asked.

"I could drive." Kobbs grunted out.

"No. That's very nice of you…both of you, to offer. But I'm doing fine now. Thank you."

Not another word was spoken until they reached the downtown corner of Fifth Street and Union, and pulled up to the Gaslight Village Apartment Complex.

"Now, I want you to remember," Kobbs grunted again. "That directory was two years old. She might not still be living here."

Ellis jammed the car into park and jumped out. He looked over the outside of the building. It was a well-done refurb. It had a kind of posh old look, with large windows facing the lights of the street. It felt like the right place. The others climbed out and stood next to him. "This looks like...ahh...what I saw in my vision. This looks right."

With the others in tow, he headed into the new glass double-doored foyer and scanned the rows of entry buttons for the name Lee. There were many more buttons than one would have expected in a building like this. Though Ellis remembered the apartment was small, the building itself must be very deep.

It was Kazi, the non-native English-speaking member of the group who found it first. He pointed to a button labeled, "K. Lee. Here."

Ellis reached over and slammed it with his hand. It let out a low, cranky buzz. There was no response.

He buzzed again. Still no response.

Ellis pushed the button in rhythmic buzzes, not stopping, hoping to annoy her enough to react, but after a couple minutes there was still no response.

"What do we do now?" Julia asked.

"This," Kobbs said, and he pushed a lone button under a sign that read "Building Super."

Again there was no response, so Kobbs pushed the button and held it down until an irritated voice cried out in an overhead speaker. "What the hell do you want?"

Kobbs released the button and looked up. "We need to be let into apartment number..." He looked over to Ellis.

"Oh," Ellis said, realizing he hadn't noticed what number apartment she lived in. "Ahhh." He glanced at the number next to the button he'd been pressing. "315."

"315." Kobbs repeated.

"Are you kidding me right now?" The voice from above said. "Do you honestly think that strange people just show up here in the middle of the night, ask to be let into an apartment, and I just open the door for them?"

"Sir, listen," Ellis said. "I have reason to believe..."

"Get the hell out of my lobby."

"Yes sir, but." Ellis stammered. "Sir? Sir?" There was no answer.

"Dickhead, she may be killing herself!" Julia screamed. The three men looked over at her. "What? This is serious."

"Hell no," Kobbs said. "I didn't freeze my ass off on Christmas Eve to be ignored." He reached over and leaned against the button until the voice came on the speaker again.

"Stop that. I can see you haven't left yet."

Kazi patted Ellis's arm and pointed to a small dark dome in the ceiling above the doors. Ellis stepped over and addressed the camera. "Sir, I have reason to believe that Miss Kimberly Lee in apartment 315 is depressed and may be attempting suicide at this very moment. We've tried buzzing her room but she doesn't answer. All we want is to be let into her room and check on her. If she's fine we'll leave, no harm done."

"It's a free country. People are allowed to kill themselves if they want."

Julia gasped and covered her mouth with her hand.

Kobbs growled. The old rancher shoved Ellis aside, and looked up at the camera. "Actually, you mental midget, suicide is currently illegal in all 50 states. So, if she is found dead tomorrow, and they determine time of death to be after this very minute, I'll see that you're brought up on charges for aiding and abetting her death. You'll be an accomplice, and it will go from a suicide to manslaughter. How does fifteen years hard time sound to you? And all because you were too damn lazy to drag your fat ass down here and let us in."

There was a long pause. Then finally, "Ahhh, shit." The voice above said. "Hold on. I'll be right out."

Kobbs looked over at Ellis. "Sorry, about the pushing thing, there."

Ellis smiled. "Don't give it another thought." He was now very pleased the old man had decided to join them.

Julia whispered. "Is suicide really illegal in all fifty states?"

Kobbs grumbled. "I have no idea. Nor do I know how many years you get for manslaughter." The old man shrugged. "But I was sure he didn't know either, so…"

A door opened in the right side of the lobby. A man stepped out wearing a white t-shirt, flannel pajama pants, and black socks. He had greasy brown hair, three days-worth of beard, and a belt around his waist with a huge ring of keys connected to a retractable chain. He pulled the ring up, selected one, and opened the glass doors. "All right, let's get this over with so I can get back to my movie. You're lucky it's a commercial."

The four of them followed the man to the elevator, climbed in, and watched as the doors squeaked slowly closed. Ellis's stomach lurched. If he would have known the elevator was going to be so slow, he would have taken the stairs.

Not a word was spoken the entire time the elevator crept up to the third floor. When it hit three, it eased to a slow stop, then dinged a second later. It was several more seconds for the doors to start to slide open. "This is bullshit," Ellis said. "Are these the same damn elevators that were installed with the building in 1882?" He pushed the doors open with both his hands and jumped off.

"Keep your pants on, man," the super said. "I'm the one with the key anyway."

Ellis didn't wait. He ran down to apartment 315 and pounded on the door with both fists. "Miss Lee? Miss Lee, are you there? We just want to make sure you're all right."

The super sauntered up, whispering harshly. "Hey, dummy, keep it down. We don't allow a ruckus like that, even in the light of day."

A door across the hall opened and clunked against its own chain. A gray-haired, wrinkled face appeared in the crack about four feet off the floor, with all the creases stretched into sincere concern.

"I'm sorry for the disturbance, Mrs. Rubin," The super said, holding his hands out to calm her. "I've got it under control."

Mrs. Rubin let the door close slowly and quietly.

The super turned and frowned at Ellis. He spoke in a low gravely tone. "I'm doing you a favor and breaking a whole set of rules by letting you in here. You need to keep it down."

Ellis nodded, and pointed to the door. "Understood. She's not responding. Can you please hurry and open up the door?"

The super shook his head, selected the correct key from his respectably sized ring, and looked at the four of them. "I will go in and check on her. You stay here. I'll let you know what I find."

When they all nodded their consent he turned and unlocked the door. As soon as the latch clicked, Ellis rushed past him, followed by Kazi, Julia, and Kobbs.

Ellis flipped on the light by the door, ran down the little hall, past the ferret tubing on the floor, and stopped at the open bedroom. Kimberly Lee lay in her bed with her covers up over her shoulder, looking as peaceful as a sleeping baby. "Miss Lee?" Ellis said. But she did not open her eyes, nor respond in any way.

Ellis felt his stomach go cold. They were too late.

Kazi pushed his way into the room and ran over to her side. He turned on the lamp on the night stand and began to examine her. "She has pulse. Very weak. But there is pulse." He opened her eyes and peered into them. "She needs help. Quickly."

"Oh my God," Julia said, hands over her mouth trembling in the bedroom doorway.

"I'm calling 911," Kobbs said. He pulled out his phone and walked back into the living room.

Ellis noticed an empty pill bottle on the nightstand, with the white cap sitting next to it. He picked them up and examined them. The edge of the cap was rough. When he realized there were small little teeth marks dug into it, his hands started trembling.

"Ambulance is on its way," Kobbs said.

Ellis looked up, and then past him, out into the hall.

"What is it?" Kobbs asked.

Ellis ignored him. He walked out of the room, opened the closet door in the hallway, and rolled out a large ferret cage with a small, frightened ferret inside, curled into a shivering ball in the corner of the lowest level.

Julia stepped over and knelt down. "Awww, poor little guy."

Kobbs appeared to Ellis's left. Ellis pointed to the cage. "That's what a ferret looks like."

15

The super had gone down to wait at the front entrance to let the EMTs in when they got there.

Kazi sat next to Kimber and monitored her until help arrived. When Ellis asked about her, Kazi shook his head and said, "Pulse is weak and she is very cool." He touched her forehead with the back of his hand. "This is very bad. They must hurry."

Ellis looked at the young woman lying in the bed. Wondered how someone so young, so pretty, with so much to offer and a whole life ahead of her, could feel so lost. How could she have so little hope for the future that this was truly her only option?

"Oh, my God." Julia cried out from the other room. Ellis walked out to see what was wrong, and found Julia hunched down at the desk in the kitchen, reading the laptop screen. When he entered the room she stood, put her hand on her heart and turned to him, eyes glassy with tears. "This is breaking my heart."

"What did you find?" Kobbs asked from the couch. Hudu was lying on his chest, and he was comforting the little ferret by lightly scratching the top of its head. Hudu had finally calmed down.

"I found her note," Julia said. "She typed it here on this laptop, and left it for whoever found her, to read."

"What's it say?" Kobbs asked her.

"Oh my gosh, I don't know if I can get through it again." Julia bent down to the screen, took a breath and began to read the note aloud. Kazi appeared in the doorway to listen.

Sirens wailed outside, growing closer and then winding down. Ellis went to the window and saw the super rush out to the vehicle. Two EMTs, one black man and one white woman, got out of the ambulance, walked around to the back and pulled out a gurney with equipment stacked on it.

Another siren wailed, rounding the corner. It was the police. He didn't know why the police showed up, but thought it was probably routine whenever a call like this came in regarding suicide. They had to make sure everything was on the up and up.

"That is just sad," Kobbs said, when Julia had finished reading. "This poor girl really needs help."

Ellis turned to see Julia wiping her eyes, and Kazi staring at the floor. Then realized, "Kazi." He pulled his car keys out of his pocket and threw them to the African. "Can you drive?"

Kazi caught the keys and nodded, confused.

"The police are here, which means you can't be."

"Why can't he be?" Kobbs asked.

"Because he's an illegal immigrant." Ellis said.

Kazi's eyes grew wide.

Ellis walked over to him and ushered him to the door. "Don't stress about it, they're going to be a minute with that elevator so damn slow. Just take the stairs and get out of here. Drive the car down the block and wait until the police and ambulance leave, then come get us."

Kazi nodded and ran down the hall and through the stairway door just as the elevator dinged.

When the elevator doors slid open, the super jumped out and pointed in the direction of the room. "This way. C'mon." He was shaken up now and couldn't get help for Kimber fast enough. Perhaps he was truly scared by what Kobbs had said in the lobby.

The two EMTs followed him, pushing their gurney. An African American police officer brought up the rear.

When they entered the apartment, the super ran into the bedroom. Ellis handed one of the EMTs the pill bottle. "This is what she took."

"Okay, thanks," The EMT said, and they breezed on through to the bedroom, followed by the police officer.

Ellis watched them go and sighed. At that point he knew he'd done everything he could, and he was satisfied.

Then he realized something.

His eyes scanned the entire apartment. The kitchen counter, which had been covered with dirty dishes and sticky spills, was clean and shiny. All the dishes had been washed and put away. There was not even one dish left in the drainer. The living room, which had been stacked with pizza boxes, take-out containers, empty liquor bottles and beer cans, was now neat, tidy, and clean. There wasn't a single item left that didn't belong there, no dust on any surface, and the magazines on the coffee table were positioned perfectly, even with the edges of the table. The place was immaculate.

He walked back to the bedroom and saw that the mountains of clothes were gone. Nothing was on the floor, and vacuum cleaner lines were visible in the shag of the bedroom carpet.

The EMTs were working on Kimber, taking vitals, running IV's. The woman looked up to the super, and asked, "Do you know how long ago she ingested the pills?"

The super shrugged.

"It's been less than an hour," Ellis said.

All eyes turned to him. "How do you know that?" The policeman asked.

"The place was a mess," Ellis said. "It's all clean now. Everything is all clean. It had to have taken her at least two hours to take care of everything. So…"

The policeman walked over and pulled out a notebook. "What is your name, sir?"

"I'm Ellis Porter."

"And how do you know the victim?"

"I don't know her at all," Ellis said. "I've never met her before."

"But you were in this apartment less than three hours ago?"

"Yes…no…not me. I wasn't here." Ellis realized he couldn't tell the officer he'd been a ferret three hours ago. "It was a vision, or a dream, or something like that."

"A vision, or a dream," The officer said.

"Yeah. I know it sounds crazy, but it all seemed very real."

"I can vouch for him," Julia said. "He had a vision about me too, and I've never met him until a little over an hour ago."

The officer nodded his head toward Julia. "And why did you go see her?"

"Because I knew where Mr. Kobbs lived," Julia answered for Ellis.

"And who is Mr. Kobbs?"

"I am," Kobbs walked in from the living room, still cuddling Hudu.

The officer looked at Kobbs, then back at Ellis. "And why did you have to go see him?"

Kobbs spoke up. "Because I had the address to this apartment at my house, in an old church directory."

The officer pointed at Ellis. "Okay, this next question is for you, and you're the only one I want to hear from. Got it?"

Ellis nodded.

"If you saw this place in a vision, why didn't you just drive here? Why did you drag all of these other people into it?"

"Because I only saw it from the inside. I never saw the building from the outside, so I didn't know the address, or even what it looked like. I had no way to find it."

"So why did you look?" The officer asked.

"Because I read the…" Ellis paused, and clarified. "In my vision, I saw her typing something, and I was able to read it. She has a suicide note on the computer in the kitchen. And then I saw her getting pills. And that's about it."

"That's all you saw in your…" The officer twirled his pen in the air. "…vision."

Ellis nodded. "Yes. And I knew I had to get here…so I went to the other places I had visions about."

"So he came to me," Julia said.

The officer scribbled more notes in his notebook and shook his head. "And you were all able to get here in time to save her life."

"Thank God. Right?" Julia said. "I mean, seriously."

"Yes, ma'am." The officer closed his notebook and slid it in his pocket. "It's a regular Christmas miracle." He clicked his pen and slid it into his shirt pocket. "But after fifteen years on the force, I'd be lying if I said I hadn't seen stranger things." He looked over at Ellis. "Mr. Porter, until she wakes up I'm going to have to ask you to stay in town in case we have any further questions."

"That won't be a problem, Officer. I have no plans to go anywhere." In fact, all he wanted to do now was go home and go to bed. With the proper medication, he could probably leverage his weariness, and sleep through to the 27th.

Within five minutes, the EMTs had IVs in Kimber, had her loaded onto the gurney, and wheeled out of the apartment.

The police officer was taking a picture of the computer screen when the super walked over to him.

"So we're good?" The super said. "I mean she's alive and all. You don't need anything more from me?"

"Unless you have information that you're not telling me."

"Oh, no sir," The super waved the officer off. "I don't know anything."

"I believe you," The officer said.

The super turned back to Ellis, Julia, and Kobbs. "Okay, you've done what you came here for. It's time to go." He frowned and looked around the room. "Hey, where's the little black fella?"

Kobbs slipped Hudu back into his cage and stood back up. "What black fella?"

The super stood, brows knitted, looking back and forth to each of their faces. Then he shrugged and ushered them all out of the room.

The door to the apartment across the hall was open and the little wrinkled face was once again peering through the crack. The super smiled and waved at her. "Everything is all settled down now, Mrs. Rubin. We're all leaving. You have a very Merry Christmas, all right?"

Mrs. Rubin frowned. "I wish you'd stop saying that to me, dickhead. I'm Jewish." She slammed her door.

"Ohhh, the mouth on you, you old bat." The super yelled. "I didn't think they spoke like that in the 1850s."

Kobbs and the police officer laughed out loud. Julia had her hand over her smiling mouth. Ellis chuckled but tried his best to hide it with a fake coughing jag.

"Oh yeah, real funny." The super said, and he stamped down the stairs. "I save a woman's life tonight, and this is the thanks I get."

Ellis followed Julia and Kobbs outside. They watched the officer get into his squad car and drive away. Once he had turned the corner, lights came on a block down the road, and Kazi drove up in Ellis's Equinox. Everyone was opening doors to get in when Ellis spoke up. "Listen. I just want to say thank you to all of you for helping me with this. I know it was strange having me show up like I did, but you all pitched in and it worked out. And I just want you all to know how grateful I am before I take you home."

"Take us home?" Julia said. "We're not going home yet. We have to go to the hospital."

"Well...no," Ellis had no desire to go to the hospital. He only wanted to go play bear and hibernate. "I mean, she's been saved and all."

"She hasn't been anything." Julia protested. "We only stopped her from dying. We haven't saved her life. Do you think she's not going to try it again?"

"Well that's fine for you, but the others..."

"The others what?" Kobbs said. "Son, you've given me the most exciting Christmas Eve I've had in years.

Yes, it's past my bedtime, but honestly, I'm not ready to call it quits yet."

Ellis looked at Kazi, hoping the African would say that Tumbili really needed him to get back or something. But he knew, out of the four of them, Kazi was the one who surely had no plans. He looked up the road and sighed. The night wasn't over just yet. He gestured to the car. "Okay. Get in."

16

"The Christmas Four," walked into the hospital. Kobbs nicknamed their strange little band on the car ride over. He'd suggested the word "quartet" to begin with but decided that sounded too much like a group of carolers, and just saying "four" had an air of mystery about it. He said they'd created a new tradition, and every Christmas Eve they should all get together, ride out, and perform one Christmas miracle.

Julia pointed to the Emergency Room check-in desk. "I'll let them know we're here for Kimber."

Ellis spotted a coffee vending machine and asked if anybody wanted some. He was aware of the irony of the moment. He was the only one who wanted to go home and go to bed, and he was the one springing for the coffee to keep everyone awake. Kobbs went along to help him carry the cups.

Ellis was feeding in dollar bills when Kobbs spoke up. "So what do you think, Porter? Was this a miracle? You know, your visions and all."

Ellis shrugged, made a selection, watched the cup drop, and hot brown liquid pour into it. He thought about the moment he woke up and Strawberry and Rhubarb spoke to him. How frightened he was at first, and then how quickly he became used to talking with them. Now, being away from them for a while, he wondered if it had really happened in the first place. Perhaps the things he saw truly were visions after all. Ellis pulled the cup, handed it to Kobbs and fed in another dollar. "I can tell you this," He said. "I'm no miracle man. Far from it."

After filling four cups of coffee they walked over to where Kazi and Julia were sitting, in the middle of the dim and empty waiting room. Julia had been talking and Kazi listening, but they quieted when Ellis and Kobbs arrived, and handed them their coffees. Kobbs sat next to Kazi and Ellis sat across from him, next to Julia.

Julia opened her mouth to say something, then closed it, opened it again, then closed it.

"Spit it out, young lady," Kobbs said.

Julia looked at Ellis then Kobbs. "Well, we were just talking…"

Ellis was fairly certain it was Julia talking and not Kazi.

"...And now that things are calmer, we've had a chance to think about how this whole night played out. And to be quite frank, it has been kind of miraculous, but a little bit creepy at the same time."

"Creepy how?" Ellis said.

Julia turned to him. "Well...you. You had these dreams about us and they all turned out to be true, but how did the dream play out? You knew things about Kimber and her apartment, details that just don't come through in an ordinary dream."

"Well, it was anything but an ordinary dream," Ellis said. "It was like I was there in the room."

"How so?" Kobbs asked.

Ellis took a sip of his hot coffee—surprisingly good for coming out of a vending machine. He thought about how he would explain his day to these three strangers so they wouldn't think he was a complete loon. But they were strangers after all, and he truly didn't need to worry about it. If they thought he was bonkers that was their issue. He turned out to be right about everything, so they couldn't deny that. "Okay, this is going to sound completely strange, but it was as if I was seeing everything through the eyes of the animals in your lives."

The three of them looked at each other. Kazi appeared to understand first. He looked back at Ellis. "You were seeing from Tumbili?"

"Yes." Ellis pointed at him. "Exactly."

"And you were seeing from the eyes of Deepak?"

"Yes."

"And you were seeing things from the eyes of Charlie?"

"No," Ellis shook his head. "Who's Charlie?"

"Charlie's my dog. He's a husky."

"No. It wasn't a dog. In your case it was a horse."

Kobbs faced looked as if it melted, "What horse?"

Ellis recalled how Kobbs held the horse's head and cried. He was almost afraid to say the name, but he had gone this far. "Mr. Smith."

Now Kobbs's whole body appeared to melt into the chair.

"What is it?" Julia said. "Who's Mr. Smith?"

Ellis watched Kobbs's whole demeanor change. Just mentioning the name sent him into a grief state. "Mr. Smith was a very special horse to Mr. Kobbs."

Julia looked over at Kobbs. "Was?"

Kobbs set his coffee cup down with a trembling hand, rested his elbow on the chair and propped his head up with his knuckles. In the matter of a moment, he was reduced to a weak and weary old man. His lips parted and he spoke slowly. "I had a grandson. Caleb. Bright kid. Always smiling. Always laughing. Always talking.

Couldn't be quiet." He gestured toward Julia. "In a way, you remind me of him."

Julia's back straightened.

"He was full of life. The kind of kid you wanted to be around as much as possible."

Julia smiled, and relaxed again.

"He lived in Georgia with my son and his wife, but in the summers he would come and stay with us on the ranch. I gave him a horse that he named Mr. Smith, after the old movie, 'Mr. Smith Goes to Washington.' You know, the one with Jimmy Stewart."

Julia and Kazi shook their heads. "I'm sorry, sir. I don't." Julia said.

"I've seen it," Ellis said. "Great movie."

"Boy, he loved that movie." Kobbs chuckled. "He watched it one afternoon on TV, and then we had to buy it for him because he wanted to watch it over and over. It got in his head; he wanted to go into politics after watching that movie for the umpteenth time." Kobbs shook his head and smiled at the memory. "Anyway, when he stayed with us a few years back, the foal came along, and I told Caleb it was his horse. He named it Mr. Smith, and the damn thing was, it seemed the horse was the only thing that pulled him away from the movie. He loved that horse and took really good care of it." Kobbs stopped talking. He just shook his head continuously.

"What happened to Caleb?" Julia asked.

"Last June. The last week of school I think, he was riding his bike home. He crossed a street, and some damn teenager was texting while she was driving and ran him over. Missed the stop sign completely. Never even slowed down."

Julia gasped.

Kazi reached over and patted him on the back. "I'm so sorry, Mr. Kobbs. That's very horrible."

Ellis knew the story. It happened just as Strawberry and Rhubarb had said it did. There were some details they left out though. "That must have been hard on your wife too."

Kobbs sighed. "I'm not so sure she's aware of it yet. She has Alzheimer's and last February I had to send her to live in an assisted living home." He looked up at Ellis and Julia, eyes red, sounding defensive. "I didn't have any choice. I had a ranch to tend to, and she would have these spells where she wouldn't know where she was. She'd get scared and run out into the winter weather with just her nightgown on. We were all afraid she was going to end up getting lost and freezing to death."

"It's okay," Ellis leaned forward and patted the man's forearm. "It sounds like you made the right choice."

"Do your kids come and visit her?" Julia asked.

Kobbs shrugged. "Only have the one, and he's gone AWOL. Nobody has seen or heard from him since the funeral. He and his wife divorced and I don't hear from her either."

"And what about Mr. Smith?" Kazi asked. "You looked sad when Mr. Porter said his name."

Kobbs looked over at Kazi. "This morning I went out to check on him, and he was lying down in his stall. He was wiggling and kicking, and I knew it wasn't good. I called the doc over and he confirmed what I'd feared; the horse had a terminal case of colic. Mr. Smith had to be put to sleep this morning. He was all I had left of Caleb. All I had left of anybody. In less than one year my whole family is gone." Kobbs covered his face with his hands and wept quietly.

"Oh, poor dear," Julia said. She jumped up and stood over by Kobbs, rubbing the old man's shoulder while he struggled to collect himself. She looked over at Ellis. "Did you know this?"

"No," Ellis said. "I only knew about the horse, and his grandson. I'm sorry, Mr. Kobbs." He pulled tissues out of a box on the table next to him and handed them over.

Kobbs took them. Dabbed at his eyes. "It's all right. I'm sorry, you guys. I don't mean to put a damper on your Christmas." He blew his nose loudly.

Before anyone had a chance to tell him he was fine, a white male nurse with a blond 'fro stepped up. "You're here for Kimberly Lee?" When they all nodded, he spoke again. "The doctors wanted me to tell you that they have performed a gastric lavage and that she is stable."

"What is that?" Julia asked.

"They cleaned out her stomach," Kazi said.

"Yes. That's essentially it," the nurse said. "He pumped her stomach. She's still unconscious and we want to keep her here until she wakes up and we can assess her and be sure there's no permanent damage. Are there any questions?"

The four glanced back and forth at each other.

"Okay then, you're welcome to go back and sit with her if you'd like."

They thought about it and Julia spoke up, "I don't think so, we're going to be talking and we won't want to disturb her."

"All right then," The nurse smiled at them. "I'll come and let you know when she wakes up and you can go see her then."

"Thank you," Julia said.

The nurse walked away, and Julia sat back down. "So you were seeing through Deepak?"

"Are we going to do this with everybody?" Ellis asked.

"Well we're definitely doing it with me," Julia said. "Deepak is the only animal I have, so I'm assuming you saw through his eyes."

Ellis nodded.

"You named the damn goat Deepak?" Kobbs said.

"Yes. He helps with my yoga, and he helps me center myself." She turned back to Ellis. "What did you see?"

"I saw Brad."

Julia rolled her eyes. "Not the most stellar part of the day."

"It looked like you handled him pretty well."

"Who's Brad?" Kobbs asked.

Julia sat back in her chair. "A guy from my past who will remain there, whether he likes it or not."

Ellis looked over at Kobbs. "He doesn't like it."

"What else did you see?" Julia asked.

Ellis shrugged. "I saw you cry when your toilet got plugged."

"Oh, yeah. That."

"Was Brad the man in your life who took care of things like that?" Kobbs asked her.

"No, Brad took care of only Brad things." Julia crossed her arms. "And I'm done with the man thing anyway."

After a pause Kobbs asked, "Woman?"

"No. I'm solo."

"So you're single right now then?" Ellis asked.

"No. I feel the word 'single' implies that you're eventually looking to be 'couple.' I no longer have any desire to couple up with anybody, so if I have to put a word to it, I call myself 'solo.' It means 'one' and 'one only.'"

"Got your heart broken?" Kobbs said.

"Not at all. In fact I ended up doing the breaking. That's what Brad was so upset about." Julia took a sip from her coffee, set it back down on the table and continued. "I did the dating thing, had lots of boyfriends, and even allowed myself to get engaged to Brad. None of that made me happy. I just don't couple well. I appreciate companionship, but that's it. I don't share my life well. It causes severe anxiety in me. As our wedding day grew closer, I was getting sick more and more often. I ended up in the hospital a couple of times because I wasn't eating, and I grew weak and passed out. Everybody called it 'cold feet.'" She made quotes with her fingers. "But I realized that it was more. And it wasn't just with Brad, it was with everybody I ever dated. Sure I could love them and care for them, I just couldn't make the leap to couple with them. So I finally decided I'm not going to be something, or someone I'm not, just because that's the way everybody else does it. So I broke off the engagement, quit my boring job at the dentist's office, bought a barn, and I've never been happier."

"Until your toilet gets plugged," Ellis said.

Julia looked at him, eyes narrowing.

Ellis raised his hands in surrender. "Just asking because I'm curious. I've never met a 'solo,' so I'm confused. If you're happy being alone, why do you cry when something simple happens like a clogged toilet?"

"Just because I choose to live alone, doesn't mean I don't get lonely. And yes, sometimes it does get hard, and things like a clogged toilet can highlight that. Especially when your toilet clogs on Christmas, and you know everyone else in the world has someone who will just walk in there and unclog it for them. But I can't be in a relationship just to have a handyman, or someone to talk to one or two days out of the year. Everyone needs companionship, and that's why I have Deepak. Yes, he helps out with the classes, but he's my buddy too. And I can be very giving of myself. I just can't be giving to one person only. I have to have several people in my circle. I think that's why my business has worked out so well. When they walk into my house to work out, they really are walking into my house. I treat them like family, I help them relax, get in shape, they feel comfortable and cared for, and they come back."

"Solo, huh?" Ellis thought about it for a minute. "I like it." That's what he was now.

Kobbs turned to Kazi. "What animal do you have?"

Kazi looked over at Ellis. "Tumbili."

Ellis smiled. "Yes. Tumbili."

"What is Tum...what did you call it?"

"Tumbili. He's a spider monkey," Ellis said. "And our African friend here is fearless. He stitched up a bleeding tiger today."

"You what?" Julia said.

"What the hell do you do?" Kobbs said.

Kazi blushed at the attention. "I work and live at the Billing Park."

"The zoo?" Kobbs said. "How do you live there?"

"Yes," Kazi nodded. "I have a cot in back of the monkey house. Mrs. Rikter has been very kind."

"Did she help you get into the country?" Julia asked.

"No," Kazi said. He looked back and forth at everyone nervously.

"Just tell us," Kobbs said.

"I have a feeling I know why he's here," Ellis said. He could see Kazi was reluctant to say too much and he wanted to help him out.

"Why is that?" Kobbs said.

"I believe Kazi is gay. And in his country you can go to prison for that."

"What?" Kobbs said. "Are you gay?"

Kazi stared at Ellis, eyes wide. He started taking deep breaths, and trembling.

"Oh, sweetie. No, no." Julia leaned forward, and took his hand. "You have nothing to fear here. We're here for you."

Ellis leaned forward as well, and looked Kazi in the eye, speaking calmly to him. "Kazi, I'm not accusing you. I'm only trying to understand you. Being gay is not a crime here. You're safe with us."

Kazi grasped Julia's hand with both of his and brought his sad eyes up to hers.

"That's it, Kazi. We're right here."

"Awww hell, son." Kobbs patted Kazi's shoulder. "Of course we're here. Help us understand what's going on."

Kazi took several breaths and spoke quietly. "I worked as an animal doctor for a great wilderness park in my country of Kenya. Myself and Oringo...my friend. We became very close, Ori and I. But nobody knew. Nobody was supposed to know. It's not allowed for men to be close like that. One day we rescued a lion cub. We didn't think it would live, but we cared for it for three days. When the cub finally woke up, Ori and I cheered. We were very proud. We hugged, and then Ori kissed me. Our boss walked in at that time. He saw us, and he walked right out. We knew we were in trouble.

We had to run. I went home to my house to pack. Ori went to his. When he came over to get me, the police arrested him, right in front of my house. I saw it out my window. I grabbed one small bag and ran out the back door, got in my car and drove away. When I got to the coast, I sold the car for money to get onto a freighter boat. That is how I made it to America."

"What about Ori?" Ellis asked.

Kazi wiped at his eyes. He spoke again with a quivering voice. "He is now in prison. He will be there for 14 years." Kazi sniffed and put his arms over his face. "I will never see him again."

Julia looked at Kobbs and Ellis and mouthed, "Oh my God."

It took only a few moments for Kazi to regain his composure. He glanced up at them, then dropped his gaze to his lap. "I am very sorry for acting like this."

"Son, don't say another word." Kobbs said, patting him on the shoulder. "We've all got our crosses to bear and yours seems extra heavy."

Kazi looked over at him, brows furrowed in confusion, but thanked him politely none-the-less.

The conversation ebbed, and everyone sat silently in the quiet waiting room.

Ellis felt the pressure. It was now his turn to speak. He was the one who was supposed to fill the muted void. Each member of this new group opened up, shared their innermost feelings, but he couldn't. He wouldn't. The thought of even trying to talk about Cheri, made his stomach twist. He knew he couldn't discuss what they had, or how his life without her was like living in a constant gray fog.

Julia looked over at him first, expectant. Then Kazi's eyes met his, as if saying, "You were the one who told my secret, now it's time to tell yours." And finally Kobbs shot him a stare. They were clearly waiting, trusting his heart would open and his story would be coming soon.

Parting his lips, Ellis contemplated giving them something, some little nugget to satisfy their craving, "I...." But nothing could come out. His heart closed down. "Can't."

"You can't what?" Julia asked him.

Something akin to panic hit Ellis and he jumped from his seat. There was a fight or flight reflex taking hold, and he'd never been much of a fighter. "This is not for me. I'm sorry, perhaps you can get a cab, or an Uber or something." He darted for the exit. "It was nice to meet you all."

"Ellis," Julia called.

"Hey there," came Kobbs scratchy voice.

But Ellis hit the door, ran out into the bitter cold night, hurried to his car, and sped away.

He never looked back

17

The neighborhood was much darker in the early hours of Christmas morning. A few houses kept their lights on all night, but the majority of the homeowners let their electric bills dictate how long to remain lit each night. Ellis parked in his driveway and walked into his house, glancing over his shoulder briefly to see if Perry Mueller was still waiting to yell at him again. The Mueller house was dark too.

Ellis closed and locked the door then collapsed into his chair, exhausted. For some reason it felt like days since he'd been there. He rested his head on his hand and recalled the events of the night. It had been an amazing experience, meeting the three individuals who had been unaware of his visits that day, teaming up with these strangers to save the life of another young woman. And even though he left them stranded at the hospital, after the night they had, and what they accomplished, he was proud of himself.

"You ought to be ashamed of yourself," The old woman voice of Strawberry said.

Ellis looked around to see her strut in from the bedroom, followed by tired, old Rhubarb. "Oh, now you're going to talk to me? Where were you hours ago, when I really needed you? No. When Kimber really needed you? If you would just have told me where to find her in the first place, I probably would've gotten to her before she even took the pills and I wouldn't have even had to bother Kazi, Julia, and Kobbs."

"Don't talk to us like we're the disappointments here, Ellis Wayne Porter," Strawberry said.

Ellis's breath caught in his throat. The only person whoever called him by his full name was Cheri, when she truly had a point to make.

"We played our part. You fell short on yours."

"How do you figure?" Ellis said. "Kimber is alive right now because of me."

"Yes. But alive isn't living, is it?" Strawberry paced back and forth in front of him. "But you know that already, don't you, Ellis? You've been alive for an entire year, but you haven't *lived* a single day of it."

"Let's not get back to that again," Ellis said. "I've played your damn game all day. And in the end, I followed through and saved that young woman's life. I think today, we both lived."

Strawberry continued to pace. "But on December 26th nothing will have changed."

"What do you mean, nothing will have changed?"

"It is just as Julia said. All you did was stop her from dying. You have yet to do anything to save her life. And you couldn't even wait an entire night before you had to run back and crawl in your hole."

Ellis could feel his face grow red. "You better shut your mouth right now or you'll be sleeping out in the cold."

"It's too bad that wasn't an option, like ten years ago," Rhubarb said. He looked over at Strawberry. "Calm down, cat. Let the dog handle this one. We are the loving pets, anyway."

Strawberry sat and looked away. "Fine. You handle him then."

Rhubarb walked over and sat at Ellis's feet. "This wasn't just about stopping Kimberly Lee from taking a few pills. Otherwise you would have been sent straight to her to begin with, and you would have been given the chance to go talk to her before she even took the top off the bottle. You didn't just save one life today, you saved many more. At least you were on track to, before you gave up and ran back home."

"I don't know what you mean. How did I save many lives?"

"Without you in their lives, those four were on a collision course with bad fortune. Kimber would have succeeded in killing herself, ending the chance for her own happiness in the future with a husband and three children who would have been blessings to her life."

"Is that what's going to happen to her?"

"Well, not anymore," Rhubarb said. "Not since you left. But it was headed in that direction."

"Don't say that. I don't deserve that pressure. People need to be responsible for their own actions."

"It's not just she who's affected," Rhubarb said. "Kazi is destined to be discovered. He will be picked up by immigration officials and deported. When he is returned to Kenya, he will be imprisoned for his 14-year sentence. Laura Rikter will lose her job for trying to do the right thing, and the zoo will pay a hefty fine. Mr. Kobbs will continue to find the solution to his pain with hard liquor. This will lead to a few bad decisions at the height of inebriation. The worst of which is the midnight horse ride across his property, where he is too drunk to stay in the saddle. He will fall and break his neck, and no longer be the strong, steady force that his wife and his son desperately need him to be."

"That's awful," Ellis said. "But what about Julia? She's the strongest of us all."

"Julia is the neediest of them all. But she needs you the most, and you need her too."

"I don't need her."

"You both are determined to not need anyone in your lives. But not needing anyone is easier when you have someone to depend on. You can each be a supporting side of a lean-to. Without you, Julia won't have the strength to be there for everyone else like she dreams of doing. Things like clogged toilets will finally become too much to deal with, and she will get married out of necessity and never live a happy day again."

"There are worse tragedies than that," Ellis said. "That is her decision."

"But remember the part where I said you needed her too. If you don't make the effort to get out and live life again, be a part of something other than your own sorrow, Kate and Cassie will suffer. Kate's marriage won't last, and Cassie will drift from relationship to relationship, never finding what she needs, because she needs her father's love first."

Ellis leaned forward and stared into his dog's eyes. "This is bullshit. How do you know any of this is real?"

Strawberry tsked. "After the day you've had, you're going to ask that question?"

"So what needs to happen? Do I just have to go back down to the hospital?"

Rhubarb shook his head. "No. You have to go down to the hospital and tell them about Cheri."

"What?" Ellis felt his stomach wrench tight again. "Why would I have to bring her up?"

"Because, as the saying goes," Strawberry said. "They don't care if you care, until they know how much you care."

"That's not how the saying goes."

"It's how it goes *today*." Strawberry snapped.

Rhubarb put his paw on Ellis's knee. "You have to bring her up for two reasons. One, to let them know who you are, and how deeply you can love. They need to see that. And two, because you have to take the first, courageous step to live again. Today, Christmas Day, is the chance to share the greatest gift of your life, your wife, Cheri, with others who really could use her right now."

Ellis stared off into the distance. "I...I...don't think I can do that."

Strawberry stepped up and spoke calmly, almost lovingly. "You have always said that Cheri was the greatest light of your life and that she shone brighter at the holidays than at any other time of the year." She put her paw on his other knee. "Ellis, you are the only one who's extinguishing her light now. By not sharing her with others, you are depriving her light, killing her legacy. You are making her life meaningless."

"You once told her, you would do anything for her, even if that meant taking a bullet," Rhubarb said. "You need to do this for her. Go take that bullet, Ellis."

Ellis's feelings and fears swirled in his head and his heart. He was afraid that if he let those feelings out, he would never be able to contain them. They would devour him.

Perhaps taking the bullet would have been the much easier option.

Ellis pulled into the hospital parking lot. He looked through the window and saw Kazi, Julia, and Kobbs still sitting in the waiting room, steadfastly waiting for Kimber. They truly were remarkable people. He didn't know how to do this. He didn't have any idea what to say.

Then he looked in the other direction and noticed a red rim beginning to appear behind the row of trees along the parking lot. He smiled. "Hi, Cheri. Thanks for the help."

The three looked up at him when he entered. Not one of them looked pleased to see him.

Ellis pointed to the horizon and smiled. "The sun's thinking about coming up. We should go greet it."

"What?" Julia said. "Greet the sun? Outside? It's like twelve degrees out there."

Ellis took his seat next to her, where he had been sitting before. "It's something my wife, Cheri, used to say. She loved mornings. It was her favorite time of the day. And if she ever woke before the sun rose, she would shake me and ask me to go outside and welcome the sun with her." Ellis chuckled. "Sometimes I was so tired I could barely walk, but I always went. If I didn't go, I would've missed out on the magic." Feeling overwhelmed by the memories, Ellis choked down his grief and continued. "Cheri appreciated the smallest, simplest things in life. Found joy in just about everything. We would drink coffee, watch the sun rise together, and she would have this silly smile on her face the entire time. She'd point out when the colors changed…" Ellis realized another tear rolling down his cheek. He reached up and wiped at it, rolled it around in his fingers.

"She sounds wonderful," Julia said. "How long were you married?"

"Twenty-seven remarkable years."

"And she…died?"

Ellis nodded. "Uterine cancer. Last January."

"Kids?" Kobbs asked.

"Two ridiculously cute daughters, Katie and Cassie. In that order."

"Where are they?" Julia asked.

"Katie is engaged and works with a software company in Washington state, and Cassie is 'finding herself' in California. They wanted me to come out and visit them over the holidays, but I didn't want to. I just wanted to bury myself away and sleep through Christmas," He swirled his hand in the air. "And then all this happened and…"

"And you saved a life," Julia said. "It's been a pretty amazing Christmas Eve."

"*I* didn't expect anything like this," Kobbs said.

"Me too," Kazi added.

Ellis forced a smile. "I'm sorry I left you. I think about her, and then I have to run from the memories. I still miss her too much."

"I don't think it's possible to miss somebody too much," Kazi said.

"Missing her is the gift she gave you," Kobbs said. "If you miss her like that, it means the time you had together was special."

"Special doesn't even come close." Ellis sighed. Surprisingly, the old man could be very wise. "I wish you could have gotten to meet her. You would have loved her too. She was all the holidays wrapped up in one warm, wonderful bundle. She oozed peace and happiness, and she made every Christmas special just by being her—being a part of it all. We used to have these holiday parties the first Saturday of every December, and our house would be completely packed because people wanted to be near her. Her positive attitude was infectious."

"I feel like I am meeting her now," Kazi said.

Ellis's forced smile became real. "Last Christmas, we danced. We would dance a lot during the holidays. But that dance was different. She was so weak then. I held her upright more than danced with her. But she still smiled. And even with no hair left by then, she still looked so beautiful." Ellis gulped in his sorrow and wiped away more tears.

Julia reached over and squeezed his shoulder gently.

"Thank you," Ellis said. He rubbed his hands together and sighed. "You know, I feel like I understand this Kimber girl pretty well."

"How so?" Julia asked.

Ellis looked out at the sunrise. "It's really hard moving forward, when you know all of your tomorrows will never be as happy as all of your yesterdays."

"Now, Porter," Kobbs said. "I wouldn't go there just yet. You're still a young man, not old and crotchety like me. You could still meet someone."

"I wouldn't do that to anybody," Ellis said. "It wouldn't be fair. I'd always be judging her against Cheri, and nobody can live up to perfect." He looked over at Julia. "I liked what you said about 'solo.' I think you're on the right track there. I think I'm a solo now too."

Julia smiled. "Welcome. We can be solo together."

A tall African American doctor stepped up to them. "You are the folks here with Kimberly Lee?"

"Yes," Julia said.

"I'm Dr. Warner. I wanted to let you know, she's awake, and she's *not* very happy about it."

18

"Should we go back and talk to her?" Ellis asked the doctor.

"Well, I wanted to talk to you first." Dr. Warner slid a chair around and sat, facing all four of them. "When we have an obvious suicide attempt, especially at Christmastime, we don't like to discharge individuals without a support system. That usually means psychiatric care, or a family member. Are any of you family?"

"Oh, trust me," Julia said. "After today, this Kimber is going to think we are. And I've just now become her overbearing older sister."

"I see." Dr. Warner looked at each of them. "I can appreciate you bringing her in, and your good intentions in the early hours of Christmas morning. But if you're not related, how can I be sure that on

December 26th, you won't wave good-bye and tell her to have a nice life. That won't do her any good at all."

"That's a great question, Doctor," Kobbs said. "And I don't know if any of us have an answer that will satisfy you entirely. I will say this though, something very special happened last night—not just the fact that we managed to save this young lady's life, but in the manner that it happened. The adventure last night, along with the time we had right here in the waiting room, has bonded this group in a way you can't understand. And when Miss Julia says Kimberly Lee is now our family, she means it. We won't let you down…or more importantly, Kimberly."

The doctor looked at each of them in turn. "Do you all feel the same way he does?"

"I do," Ellis said, surprising himself. He knew, even before any of the others in the room, that something special had happened. And he also knew that if he were to tell Cheri about it, she would make sure that Kimber felt like an adopted daughter. So that is what he would do. "The only other family she has is her mother, who doesn't live close by, and who is too wrapped up in her own life to be much support anyway." He looked at the other three who were staring at him. He shrugged. "You know how I know."

Dr. Warner looked reluctantly convinced. "Okay, I'll trust you. I hope for her sake you stay committed to this." He stood, and the others stood with him. "I'll take you back."

They followed Dr. Warner through the double doors, into the maze of hallways that comprised the Emergency Department. There were a handful of nurses and doctors standing at the desk. They all looked over and nodded as the group passed by.

Dr. Warner led them around another bend then stopped at a room with the door slightly ajar. "Wait a second. Let me just tell her you're here." He entered the room and closed the door behind him. It wasn't a full minute before the door opened again and Dr. Warner emerged. "Okay," He held the door open for them.

Ellis followed Julia into the room. Kimber lay in bed, inclined slightly, with an IV in her arm and wires connected to a monitor that beeped softly behind her. She raised her head when they entered. Her hair was a mess, and she scowled at them.

"Hi, Kimber," Ellis said.

"Who are you people? And why the hell do you think it's okay to interfere in other people's lives?"

Julia wagged a finger at her. "Oh no, girl. We," She gestured to the four of them. "...do *not* interfere in the lives of others. We do, however, interfere in the deaths of others. Especially when the person who is dying is way too young to die and has so much to live for."

"Okay. Well great. You did a great thing for Christmas. Woohoo. You saved my life. Now go away, and don't bother me anymore."

"There's a problem with that," Kobbs said. "You see, I just promised the doctor that we were going to stick to you like glue from now on. So we're your support system now."

"What?" Kimber's eyes grew wide and her brows knotted. "You don't even know me. I've never seen any of you before in my life. Why would you give a shit about me?"

"I'm Julia Madison," Julia pointed to each of them as she continued with her introductions. "This is the extraordinary Mr. Porter, more on that later, then you have Kazi, who actually *lives* at the zoo. And at the end there is the crotchety Mr. Kobbs. His words, not mine." She looked back at Kimber and smiled. "And now you know us."

Kimber closed her eyes tight and rolled her head back and forth on her pillow. "No, no, no, no. I don't want to know you. I want you to *go away!*" She screamed.

Kazi stepped forward and spoke in a low calm tone. "I want you to listen."

The door swung open, and Doctor Warner looked in. Ellis held his hands up to get the doctor to stop. He mouthed, "Wait."

Dr. Warner watched as Kazi sat on the edge of Kimber's bed, then he nodded and slowly, silently closed the door once more.

"You don't know them. Neither did I before last night. But I tell you this, they are good to know." His voice had a calm, relaxing, even mesmerizing quality to it. "And I believe I understand how you feel."

Ellis considered how many times Kazi had probably used that very tone to calm an angry beast in the wild. Perhaps it had even saved his life more than once. It was working on Kimber. She laid her head back, trained her eyes on him, and rested while he spoke.

"I lost everything I cared for. I lost my home, my country, even the one person I loved very much. I sleep each night on a cot in the zoo. I have nothing to wake up for the next day. Just like you, I live with pain in my heart."

The edges of Kimber's mouth turned down and tears ran from her red eyes.

Kazi took her hand. "I know what real sadness is." He pointed to Ellis. "But last night Mr. Porter, he came to find me. He said there was a girl with a ferret who needed our help and could I go with him. Then we went to see Miss Julia and told her the same thing. She came along right away. Then we went to see Mr. Kobbs, and he wanted to help very much. He helped us find your address so we could go and save you." Kazi held up her hand and patted it. "These people all have sadness in their hearts too. They have taught me that I am not alone. They are now my friends. And I know, from this day forward, they will stand by me, prop me upright if I feel like I will fall. We will all do that for you too. Everything gonna be okay."

Forcing herself not to cry, even though tears were streaming down her cheeks, Kimber shook her head and blurted out, "But, why?"

Julia took her other hand. "Because, sweetie. You're worth it."

Kimber pulled her hands back, threw her arms over her face and cried. It was a long, sorrowful, moaning cry.

Julia sat on the edge of the bed opposite Kazi. Kimber was now flanked on both sides, supported by strangers who apparently showed more concern for her than her own family and set of friends.

Julia and Kazi patted her shoulders but didn't interrupt her tears. It was as if everyone knew she needed to purge the grief. She couldn't move forward and trust them all, without the cleansing release of a good torrent of emotion.

When Kimber finally calmed to random gasps, she pulled her arms back down and looked at the four strangers around her. "Hudu?"

"That cute little guy is safe in his cage in your apartment," Kobbs said.

"Listen Kimber," Ellis said, trying his best to be calming like Kazi. "I know it's a lot to ask, to trust four strange people whom you've never even met before, but that's what we're asking you to do. They won't let you out of here today unless you go with someone who they feel has your best interest at heart. So I guess my question is, do you think giving us a chance may be a little bit better than killing yourself?"

Kimber smiled, then nodded.

"Oh my gosh," Julia said. "Look at how adorable she can be when she smiles."

"Pretty as a Christmas present," Kobbs said.

The four of them applauded, and Kimber covered her face, this time to hide the blushing.

The door opened and Dr. Warner poked his head in again. Ellis turned to him. "I think we're ready to go, Doc."

Dr. Warner looked at Kimber. "Miss Lee, do you feel comfortable being released into the care of these individuals?"

She looked over at him and smiled. "Yes. I think I do."

Dr. Warner nodded. "Okay then, I'll get someone in here to get you unhooked and discharged."

It was a much more relaxed atmosphere when the nurse came in to get Kimber set to go. She asked about how they knew she was in trouble, and Ellis went into his vision story again.

"It got so weird," Kimber said. "After I typed my note on the computer, Hudu flipped out and went crazy. It was like the poor little guy read the screen and wanted to stop me."

Julia looked over at Ellis, brows furrowed, like she figured out more than he'd let on.

"That is weird," Ellis said. "But I like the name, Hudu."

"So do I," Kimber said. "It's a Korean word. It means, walnut. So I call him my little nut-buddy."

"You Korean then?" Kobbs asked.

Kimber nodded.

Julia turned back to her. "I was thinking that Hudu and you could come stay with me at my yoga barn for a while. I definitely have the room, and that way you won't have to feel alone."

"You live in a yoga barn?" Kimber asked. "Be careful. I may not move out."

Ellis stepped back against the wall, and watched the four people in front of him, thought about what Strawberry and Rhubarb had said about them. He looked at Kobbs, pictured him lying dead on the ground with a broken neck, Kazi behind bars in some Kenyan prison, Julia, unhappily wed. Was that truly their destiny without him in their lives? It was strange, but just as they had relayed to the doctor, and then to Kimber, he had to admit, he'd begun to realize a connection with these people. It was like they were meant to be together this Christmas. So being together after Christmas wouldn't be so bad. There was a comfort here. They'd already seen each other at their worst. It would be interesting to see them at their best. "You know what to do," He could hear Cheri's voice say. "So do it." It was as if she was standing right next to him, elbowing his ribs, getting him to do the right thing—the thing he knew he was supposed to do. "Ellis Wayne Porter." There it was—all three names. She was serious now. "What are you waiting for? You're the one who started all of this, so take charge like the man I know you are, and do it."

"I have a question for you," He said. It was so loud he even surprised himself. "I don't have anything in the house to eat, except cereal. And I don't even have one single decoration out, but..." He looked at them and sighed. "But it would be great if you would join me anyway, and we could all spend Christmas together."

All four looked at him, and then at each other.

He shrugged. "I thought it might be nice. I could pick up some frozen pizzas at the gas station or something."

"You know what?" Kobbs said. "I have the perfect wine to pair with gas station frozen pizzas."

Julia patted Kimber on the shoulder. "What do ya say? Want to help me decorate his place?"

Kimber smiled. "Thank you. I think I would like that."

Kazi shrugged. "I will be happy to be there."

19

When they walked out of the hospital, the sun had already risen. It shone down on the fresh snow from the night before, making it glisten, and adding little reflections of color to the glaring white.

They piled into Ellis's car and headed out of the parking lot with a plan. They would take Kimber to her apartment, with Julia, so they could pack a few things and get them over to Julia's barn, before heading to Ellis's house. Kobbs was sure some of his son's old clothes would fit Kazi, so they could be dropped off next. Then he would go to the gas station for Christmas dinner, head home, and start getting out the decorations.

But when they turned onto the main road heading out of town, Kobbs, who was in the passenger seat, spoke up. "Is it possible to take a quick detour?"

"I don't have any objection," Ellis said. "Anyone else?"

Julia was sitting right behind him in the back seat. "No. What's up?"

"I've been thinking about what Porter said earlier, and I've got someone I would love for you to meet."

Minutes later they pulled into the parking lot of the White Creek Assisted Living Residence, and parked.

"I don't know how this is going to go," Kobbs said. "But I want to say Merry Christmas to my wife, first thing. And I've just been thinking…if she were to pass away tomorrow, I would always regret not introducing you."

"Let's go meet her," Ellis said. Though he was now missing Cheri more than ever.

They all followed Kobbs in, and he walked straight to the front desk. "Merry Christmas, Mr. Kobbs," The older woman behind the desk said. "It looks like Mrs. Kobbs has a lot of visitors today."

"Just a few friends who wanted to say hi," Kobbs said. "Is she ready?"

"I believe she's dressed and is sitting in there waiting for breakfast."

"Good," Kobbs said. He gestured for them all to follow him to the left. They went down a couple halls until they came to a door that looked like all the others, except this had a slip of paper in the plastic holder that read, "Kobbs" and had hand-cut snowflakes taped around the sign.

Kobbs knocked gently and opened the door. "Hello, honey." He stepped in and waved for them to follow. "Merry Christmas, sweetheart. I wanted to be the first one to tell you that, but I'm probably not."

When they entered the room, across the already-made twin bed, they saw a gray-haired woman, wearing pink sweatpants, and a white sweater. She sat in a wheelchair, staring blankly out the window of her room.

Grabbing a chair from a table in the corner, Kobbs swung it around and placed it in front of her. That was the first time the woman noticed him. Kobbs sat down and took her hand. "Hey, Tina, I have some friends with me who wanted to meet you. Can you say hi?"

Tina, yanked her hand from his, and frowned.

"Okay. We don't have to hold hands today." He looked up at Ellis and the others. "As you might guess, some days are good, some days are not so good."

"Sure," Julia said. She stepped forward. "Merry Christmas, Mrs. Kobbs. It's very nice to meet you."

Tina Kobbs glanced up at Julia, grumbled something that was incoherent, but surely had meaning to Tina, then turned her head and looked out the window.

"Hey, honey. It's the holidays." Kobbs reached over and took her hand once more. "They're friendly people. They just want to meet you."

Tina pulled her hand back again, growled at Kobbs, and then smacked him on the top of his head.

"Oh, honey. Please, don't do that."

Tina growled again, smacked him on the head once more, and slapped him with her other hand.

Kobbs sat back, out of her reach. "Okay, sweetheart. We're going to let you be alone." He stood, put the chair back at the table, and turned to his new friends. "I'm sorry. This didn't go as well as I'd hoped."

"It's okay," Ellis said. He patted the old man's shoulder.

Kobbs looked back at his wife. The perpetually strong man was doing little to hide his sorrow. Mrs. Kobbs was very agitated, crying out, and still swinging her arms in Kobbs's direction from her wheelchair. Kobbs looked back up at them, his eyes now glassy with tears. "We need to go. She's not going to calm down with us standing around like this." He ushered them all out of the room, looked back at his wife and whispered, "Merry Christmas, Bean." Then he closed the door and marched back to the front desk. "It didn't go so well, Daisey. Someone needs to go in there and calm her down."

The woman named Daisey picked up the phone and hit a button. "Yeah, Mrs. Kobbs is agitated…"

Kobbs didn't slow down. He bolted out the door. The others had to walk nearly double-time to keep up with the old man.

When they reached the outside, Kobbs turned. "I'm sorry. That was such a bad idea. I just wanted you to see the woman I married, and whom I have loved for fifty-three years."

"It's okay, Mr. Kobbs," Kimber said.

Everyone looked at her. The young woman, stepped up to Kobbs and put her arms around him. "You are a very special man. I saw how you loved her. How much you still love her. You don't get frustrated when she strikes you. You love her through it. I'm glad we came. I know you better, and I'm happy I'm in such good company."

Kobbs sighed, uncomfortable at first, but eventually hugged her back.

Then she jerked away and turned to Ellis. "Now can we get back in the car? I'm the only one without a coat, and I'm freezing."

20

"Strawberry. Rhubarb." Ellis called to the two animals the second the front door was open. Rhubarb was lying in his basket in the kitchen. He raised his head lazily and looked at Ellis. "Hi, guy," Ellis said. Strawberry was nowhere to be seen, which meant she was under the couch. Obviously they weren't in any hurry to speak to him again. Ellis took that as a good sign.

He pulled the five pizzas out of the bag and tossed them in the freezer. He didn't know what else to have with Christmas pizza, so he'd bought a family sized bag of Christmas potato chips which he tossed on the counter for now. He opened the door to the little pantry to see what else he could add to this incredible holiday feast. Right in front was a big jar of applesauce that he knew Cheri had purchased. Finding that oddly appropriate, he pulled it out and checked the expiration date. "December 28th." He smiled. "Just under the wire, babe."

Ellis heard a lazy meow and turned to see Strawberry stepping out from behind the couch, stretching and yawning. Ellis sat on the floor and snapped his fingers. "Come here, you guys." Both animals sauntered over and snuggled with him, and he scratched and petted each of them on their heads. "Are you guys going to talk to me again, or are you all done with that?" Strawberry answered by purring and nuzzling her head against his fingers. Rhubarb sat down and relaxed, enjoying the attention. Ellis chuckled. "Whether or not either of you speak to me again, I want to thank you. Last night was remarkable and it was all because of you. I'm grateful for you both. Now I've got to keep working because, you'll be happy to hear, we're having special guests over for Christmas." Ellis kissed each animal on the tops of their heads, then hopped up and made an inventory of dinner.

Main course - frozen pizza. Side course - potato chips. Salad course - apple sauce. He was missing dessert. He hadn't thought about that while he was at the gas station. He could have picked up some Hostess or Little Debbie sugary somethings with a Christmas theme. He knew he didn't have the ingredients around the house to create anything, nor did he have the time.

At that moment, standing there contemplating dessert, Ellis could have sworn Cheri was next to him again, giving him a nudge toward the front door. He walked over, opened it up and looked across the street at Perry and Ellen's house. Now he was sure Cheri was guiding him. Dessert was right across the street for the taking, but he would have to swallow his pride first. Ellis smiled. "Okay, babe." He closed the front door behind him, strolled across to the Mueller's porch, and rang the doorbell.

The door opened and Perry Mueller appeared with a big smile that melted straightaway with recognition. "What the hell do you want, Porter?"

"Merry Christmas, Perry," Ellis said, with a sheepish smile. "If Ellen is available, I'd really like the opportunity to apologize to her, and see if she still has any cookies left."

Perry crossed his arms, pursed his lips, and stared at Ellis intently for a moment before calling out, "Ellen, there's someone here who'd like to talk to you."

A moment later, Ellen Mueller appeared in the doorway in her peach robe, holding a cup of coffee. "Well, Merry..." She saw Ellis and her smile melted, just like her husband's "Oh, hi Ellis." She picked at her messy gray hair with her free hand.

"Good morning, Ellen," Ellis said. "Listen, I wanted to let you know how sorry I am for how I acted the other day. I've been in such a bad place, this being the first Christmas without Cheri and all. My mood has been so sour, to say the least, and I took it out on you. I'm ashamed of how I acted, when all you were doing was being the sweet kind Ellen I've grown to depend on. I'm hoping you can forgive me."

Ellen chuckled under her breath and picked at her hair with more determination. "Oh, Ellis. I understand. It's okay, but I thank you for saying that. Merry Christmas to you, and all."

"Speaking of Christmas," Ellis said. "Last night I met a group of strangers who, coincidently, also don't have anybody to share Christmas with. So I invited them over to my house. I managed to get together enough food for dinner, but I have absolutely nothing for dessert, so…"

It was like Ellis just clicked Ellen Mueller's smile switch. The woman's face lit up like a Christmas tree. "Would you like some cookies for them?"

"I would love to show off Ellen Mueller's famous sugar cookies, if you still have some left to share."

"Of course I do," Ellen said, giggling. "How many people?"

Ellis held up his hand. "There will be five of us altogether."

"You wait here. I'll be right back." Ellen giggled all the way into the kitchen.

Perry smiled, watching her walk away. "There's a woman who's much happier giving than receiving."

"She's a special one, Perry," Ellis said. "Cherish every day with her."

Perry looked back at Ellis, then stuck out his hand. "Thank you for coming by, Ellis. I know this has to be tough for you, but Merry Christmas anyway."

Ellis took his hand. "Thanks." Then he pulled him in for a nice tight hug. "Merry Christmas to you too, big guy."

Perry patted Ellis on the back lightly, then pulled back and crossed his arms.

Ellen came back around the doorway carrying the plate of some of the best work Ellis had ever seen. Her face could hardly contain the smile. "Here's two for each of you. But if you finish these and want more, don't be shy."

Ellis thanked her, winked at Perry, walked back to his house and dropped the cookies on the counter next to the chips. Then he headed downstairs to grab the boxes of Christmas decorations.

The first box was the tree. He remembered how nervous Cheri used to get, that it was too much for him. He liked to macho it up for her and act like it was no problem at all. But now that she wasn't there to fret, he felt a little more free to wince and chug at the task. The other six boxes were considerably lighter, containing lights, ornaments, garland, and holiday knickknacks for around the house.

The rest of the group had said they wanted to take showers and get a little sleep before they came over, but

Ellis found that even though he had been up all day and all night, he was surprisingly full of energy. He decided instead to take a shower before he started decorating. Once he was out, however, he had a change of heart. The hot water sapped his strength, and he was forced to get some sleep. The others said they would be over around 3, so he set his alarm for 2, and was unconscious mere seconds after his heavy head crushed the pillow.

The alarm buzzed in the distance, slowly dragging him out of a deep slumber. When he realized what the noise was, he reached over and shut it off. The clock said 2:05. It had taken five minutes for the alarm to wake him up. Ellis stumbled into the kitchen, slogged through getting the coffee going, then went into the bathroom to get ready.

With clothes on, teeth brushed and coffee in hand, Ellis had renewed energy to get things rolling. He walked into the living room where he had placed all the boxes, set his coffee down and flipped open the lid to the Christmas tree. Just inside, slipped in through the opening in the top, was a white envelope. Ellis pulled it out to find it said, "My Love," in Cheri's handwriting on the front. Instantly his legs felt wobbly. Ellis stumbled back to a chair and dropped into it. He sat entranced by the envelope in his shaking hand. That was Cheri's pen. Her hand had scratched out the letters that he was now staring at. She did it with him in mind. Left him her words, thoughts, something to hold on to. Even though she wasn't going to be here for the next Christmas she wanted to give him a gift anyway. A little piece of her to keep with him.

Ellis felt his cheek and pulled down a wet finger once more. He looked at the moisture on his fingertips, rolled it around, and looked back at the letter. He wanted to open it, to read her thoughts from beyond the grave. But he couldn't. If he did, they would be done, and he would have no more Cheri to look forward to. As long as the letter remained closed he still had a piece of her, something to plan on for the future. He would read it someday.

But she wrote these words for him to have. Her heart to share with him. If he didn't read them, it would be like silencing her. If she were standing before him now, he wouldn't say stop talking. I'll listen later. Why would he do that to her written words?

There was a distant knocking sound. He barely made it out.

It came again. Ellis read the front of the letter.

The front door opened a crack, and Julia's voice called to him. "Hey Porter, are you decent?" Her head peered in and she saw him. "There you are. Why didn't you answer?" She stepped in, and Kimber followed. "Look who pulled in right behind us."

Kazi and Kobbs came in. "Merry Christmas, Porter." Kobbs scratchy voice said.

Ellis barely made any of them out.

"Porter, what's wrong?" Julia said.

Ellis glanced up to her.

Julia looked back at him, concern on her face. She walked over, put her fingers on the envelope. "May I?"

Ellis held on tight. Not wanting to let Cheri go. But now these people were here. The people he'd heard Cheri's voice tell him earlier to invite over for Christmas. This was the chance to share her with them. Slowly his fingers parted and the envelope slid out of his grasp...just like Cheri had done nearly a year ago.

Julia looked at the envelope. Held it up for the others to see. Turned back to him. "Is this Cheri's?"

Ellis stared ahead at nothing. Nodded.

"Was this in one of the boxes?"

Ellis nodded again.

"It's not open. Are you going to read it?"

Ellis didn't know whether to nod or not. So he did nothing.

"Don't you think you should? Don't you think she would want you to?"

Again, Ellis didn't know what to say.

"Would you like me to read it to you?"

Ellis meant to shake his head. But he heard Cheri's voice say, "Let her, my love."

He nodded.

Julia slid the ottoman over next to him and sat down. The others found chairs and quietly took seats. Julia carefully tore open the envelope and slid out the small piece of white note paper. She unfolded it and read, "January third."

"January third?" Ellis said. "That was five days before she passed away. It was the day we took down the Christmas tree, and all of the decorations."

Julia continued. "My dearest Ellis. You have just pulled out of the driveway and gone off to the store to dutifully fetch me yet another prescription. And I'm taking the time to write you a note to sneak into a Christmas box for you to find next year. I know you love surprises, so I'm hoping this will be a good one for you."

As Julia read, Ellis did not hear her voice. He heard Cheri's beautiful sing-song sound, that he desperately missed. He stared into the distance, and pictured his beautiful, weary wife, scratching out this note to him in the very recliner he now sat in, with a weak, but devilish smile on her face.

"I can feel it, my love. This life is almost over for me. But rather than be angry or sad, all I can feel is grateful that the years I did get to live, I got to spend with you.

You have been my strong and steady when I needed support, and my cloud when I needed a soft place to land. I couldn't have asked for a better husband, and father to our daughters, and I wanted to take this opportunity to tell you that.

I am made happier by the fact that we were able to experience one last Christmas together. That is when you are at your best. Nothing makes Ellis Porter shine brighter than the holidays. Every year your energy, your enthusiasm, and your undeniable charm made each Christmas just a little more memorable than the last. I know that our parties were always so packed because everyone wanted to be around you, and feed off your delightful holiday spirit. I was so proud to live life in your shadow.

This year in particular, was terribly hard on you, but you never let it show. I could see you were determined to give me the best Christmas of my life, and I wanted to make sure you know that you succeeded. Thank you, Ellis, for once more making me feel so special to you.

I know that you have told me that you will never marry again. I can't help but selfishly say I'm happy to hear that. After all, you are MY man. But to keep someone like you away from someone else, when you could bring so much happiness into their life, is too sad to think about. I want you to know that I hope, in time, you can find someone. Someone you can share your inner light with and brighten their life as much as you have mine.

Thank you, Ellis Wayne Porter. And know that, even though I am not standing before you when you read this, wherever I am, I still love you. And I always will. Cheri."

Julia folded up the note, gently tucked it into its envelope and handed it back to Ellis.

He stared at it a moment, still processing the words that hung in his head, like pieces of art that he wanted to look into more. Study every stroke. Investigate every nuance and mix of color. He finally reached up and took the letter from Julia's hand. She smiled sweetly at him.

"That's not the way it was." He muttered.

"What do you mean?" Julia asked.

"It wasn't me that brought everyone together. It was Cheri. It wasn't my inner light. She's the one who shined. Who everyone wanted to be around. She was the one with the energy and the glow. She made my life better, not the other way around."

"That's not how she remembers it," Julia said. "And I have to tell you, given everything I've seen, I have to agree with her."

Ellis made eye contact with Julia. "What are you talking about?"

Julia gestured to the three other people in the room. "You managed to bring together all of these people on Christmas day. *You* did that."

"I was in the process of drinking myself into another stupor if you hadn't stopped by," Kobbs said. "Probably would have eventually drunk myself to death."

"I would be spending today on a cot with Tumbili," Kazi said. "I'm happier to be here."

"I wouldn't be alive, if not for you," Kimber said.

"That wasn't me," Ellis said. "That was..." He looked over at Rhubarb, who was lying in his basket, not the least bit concerned that strangers were sitting in the house. Strawberry, on the other hand, was nowhere to be found. She was probably cowering under the bed. Ellis turned back, looked at the letter, and realized he missed Cheri so much his heart felt like it was going to burst. It came out in a flood of tears. He did not cry quietly. He let out a long anguished moan. Aside from the initial weeping at her death and subsequent funeral, he had not allowed himself to cry. He had had to be strong for Katie and Cassie. All he had ever done was trickle tears. A trickle that never seemed to end. All those tears were held behind the dam of emotions he himself had built. But Cheri's letter had been the sledgehammer that shattered that dam, and the tears flooded forth, unabated.

Ellis was helpless, lost in his grief. There was nothing he could do to hold back his emotions now. And to their credit, everyone gave him his time. They somehow knew this was what he had to do. Each of them put their hands on him, gently squeezed his arm, or patted his shoulders. But not one of them said anything stupid like, 'it'll be okay.' Because it wouldn't. Cheri was now completely gone, and there would never be anyone like her in his life again.

21

When his bout of grief had passed, Ellis found himself totally drained of energy once again. If he hadn't invited his guests over, he was sure he would have just gone back to bed and slept the rest of the day away, as he had originally intended. Ironically, they were here because he'd heard Cheri's voice in his head, telling him—no, ordering him, to invite them. It was as if she knew he was going to find the note and realized he would need them around him for support.

Ellis felt grateful watching them work. They all looked quite different now, after everyone had rested, showered, and put on proper clothes. The clothes Kazi had on were a little big, but he had the sleeves and the pant legs rolled up and made them work.

Julia and Kobbs took charge, opening boxes and setting up the decorations. Kobbs had Kazi help him assemble the tree, all the while grumbling cheerily about how much better real trees were. Julia and

Kimber were hanging ribbons and setting out knickknacks in all the wrong places.

Ellis could almost feel Cheri nudge him in the ribs again and hear her tell him to get up and help them get it right. He was surprised to hear himself chuckle. He pushed up out of the chair and went into the bedroom to retrieve Cheri's phone. He turned it on, located her Christmas music list, then came back out and plugged it into the sound system. Andy Williams interrupted their chattering with, "It's the most wonderful time of the year." Then Ellis set to work helping them get everything set up correctly—the way Cheri set them up.

Everything was ready in less than an hour. Ellis informed them that was a record in the Porter household. Then, like a swarm of bees, they all headed into the kitchen to prepare the holiday feast. Kimber and Ellis got three of the five frozen pizzas in the oven. Julia found the wine glasses while Kobbs opened the wine. Kazi found a bowl and poured the potato chips into it.

"So, Kazi," Kobbs said. "You know how to take care of lions, and tigers, and bears, but do you happen to know how to take care of cows, and horses, and goats?"

"I can take care of those too," Kazi said before munching on a chip.

"Well, I happen to have a good friend who is an Iowa Senator. If we were to work on getting you a green card, do you think you might be interested in coming to work for me on the ranch?"

Kazi swallowed his chip hard. "Are you serious, Mr. Kobbs?"

"I'm serious."

Kazi ran over and hugged the old man. "I would work very hard for you."

"All right then," Kobbs said. "And I've got a little place for you to stay as well. It's not much, but it sure as hell beats a cot in the monkey house."

"That's so great," Julia said.

"Lookey there," Kobbs said, raising his glass. "I just hired me an illegal alien. A gay one too. Tina would call me downright progressive." After everyone laughed, Kobbs turned back to Kazi. "I'm assuming you have a full name, and not just the one."

"My full name is M'fanyakazi Owino."

Kobbs stared at the African dumbly.

Ellis chuckled. "That means something too?"

"It means 'hard worker,'" Kazi said, more to Kobbs than Ellis.

Kobbs shrugged. "Those are the only kind I hire." Then he sipped his wine.

"Kimber's going to start helping me with my Yoga barn," Julia said. "And, along with therapy, we're going to work on managing her depression with meditation."

"Good news all around," Ellis said. "Good for you, Kimber."

Kimber blushed.

Julia turned back to Kobbs. "And I think I'm going to be buying a few more goats from you. Deepak needs friends, and they'll help Kimber as well. She's agreed to help me take care of them."

Kobbs raised his glass. "Here's to selling more goats."

Kimber smiled. "And we're talking about having a special class, once a month, just for us five."

"What was that?" Kobbs said.

Julia giggled. "Don't worry, Mr. Kobbs, we won't break you."

Kobbs drained his glass and grabbed the bottle. "I'm gonna need to loosen up a bit if I'm gonna be turning myself into a pretzel."

"Go easy on that stuff, old man," Ellis said. "The night's just started."

"Understood," Kobbs said, and he put the bottle back down on the counter.

When the pizzas were heated, they made their way to the table that Kimber and Kazi had set. Once they were all seated, Ellis raised his glass. "I've found my someone."

"What do you mean?" Julia said.

Ellis looked at each of them and smiled. "Cheri said she hoped I could find someone to share Christmases with in the future. I've found you. You people are my new someone. I hope this is the first of many more to come."

They all raised their glasses and happily cheered the sentiment.

"And here's to Cheri Porter," Kimber said.

The others smiled and clinked glasses. "To Cheri."

Ellis took a breath. He whispered, "To Cheri." And clinked his glass too.

The song "Butterfly Kisses," rang out from the kitchen. "Hold on," Ellis said. "That's my daughters. I want them to see you." He grabbed his phone from the counter and clicked the answer button. His daughters blinked on the screen. "Hi, girls."

"Merry Christmas, Dad."

"Merry Christmas to you too." Ellis spun around so that the four people at the table could be seen behind him.

"Uhhh, Dad?" Cassie said. "Who are all those people?"

"Just a few friends I met last night. We decided to spend Christmas together." Ellis held the phone up over his shoulder. "Say hi to my daughters, everyone."

They all raised their glasses and shouted, "Merry Christmas!"

"Oh, wow. That's great, Dad." Katie said. "Well, we won't keep you. It looks like you're just sitting down to eat."

Ellis chuckled. "Thanks. We are, and I don't want to be rude. The pizzas will get cold. But I have a quick question for you before I hang up."

"Sure," Katie said. "What's up?"

"Do you girls have plans for New Year's?"

Like the book?

Please take a moment and leave an honest review. It would be greatly appreciated.

Thank you very much!

For more information on upcoming books please stop by my web page, rob-edwards.net and sign-up for updates. I will be sending out a newsletter with updates every couple of months. You can also connect with me on Facebook at @robedwardsstoryteller, on Instagram at robedwardsstoryteller, or on Twitter at @robedwards5000.

Thanks for reading!

Acknowledgments

I have been able to write a few books by this point, but this happens to be the first one I have taken the time and energy to publish.

This book (and those to follow) would not have even come to fruition without the love and support of my wife, Dayna. She has never wavered in her belief in my abilities as a storyteller, and has never tired of being my cheerleader as I have continued trying my hand at this craft. She has encouraged the voices in my head, and helped shape the worlds that I write about, as well as the people in them.

Thanks go out to my mother and my late father for instilling in a boy the idea to "Give it a shot. What have you got to lose?" My dad was a big believer in the idea that the only real failure is the failure to try. And my mom was always a big proponent of doing something or getting off the pot! (If you know what I mean.)

For my kids, Evan and Morgan, if I can give you any advice that sticks with you, please remember to always feel free to dream and reach for those dreams with all your strength.

Thanks to a great writing community in the mid-Michigan area. I have gained a great deal of advice and support from the Capital City Writers Association, the local NaNoWriMo Chapter, my writing group the Skaaldic Society, and the annual Rally of Writers.

Thanks to Anne Stanton and the Mission Point Press, for their support in this endeavor, and to C.D. Dahlquist for her incredible editing skills. Please stand by—there will be more to come!

Made in the USA
Las Vegas, NV
16 December 2021